"*Pom Squad My* into my fries. They were surprisingly good for being fictional.

"It's pretty old. Nineteen fifties or sixties, in case you couldn't tell. And, marketed toward girls, I wouldn't expect you to have heard of it."

"Is this going to happen to us whenever you read a book for the rest of our lives?"

"Well, no." She brought her straw to her lips.

I raised my eyebrows at her. I didn't think she could turn any deeper red, but I was wrong.

She swallowed. "As soon as I'm wearing my grandmother's wedding band in marriage, everything will go back to normal."

"To me?" Marriage. As in, to my real self, in the real world? My fry lodged in my throat, then continued down in a solid lump.

"Not necessarily. I think the curse, I mean legacy, would respect marriage vows. That's how this all got started, after all. My way-back great-grandmother married someone who wasn't her soul mate, so the magic passed to her granddaughter."

"And are you in a hurry for that to happen?" I searched her gaze.

Other Wild Rose Press Titles by Shelley White:

Ginger Snapped
Penny Gothic: a romance of fictitious proportions
Younger & Wylder

Square Penny: Romance and Mystery Afoot

by

Shelley White

In for a Penny, Book 2

Square Penny: Romance and Mystery Afoot

COPYRIGHT © 2022 by Shelley White

Cover Art by *The Wild Rose Press, Inc.*

The Wild Rose Press, Inc.
PO Box 708
Adams Basin, NY 14410-0708
Visit us at www.thewildrosepress.com

Publishing History
First Edition, 2022
Trade Paperback ISBN 978-1-5092-4196-5
Digital ISBN 978-1-5092-4197-2

In for a Penny, Book 2
Published in the United States of America

Dedication

To my mom, thanks for all the books and for
encouraging my love of reading.
To Atkins Memorial Library in Corinth, Maine: your
collection of Nancy Drew Mysteries was an inspiration.
Thanks.

Chapter 1

Ready? O K!

"You're absolutely sure about this book?" my best friend, Bobbie, asked for the millionth time. "Cause I'm really not a fan."

Bobbie, her boyfriend Peter, and I were ensconced in the comfy chairs in the reading nook of my shop, Penny Pincher's Used Books. We were, once again, going to be reading ourselves into the plot of an unsuspecting book, as per the family legacy (curse) I'd found myself saddled with a month ago. My grandmother's recent death left me with three things: an eclectic used bookstore, a sad heart, and an unavoidable quest to discover my soul mate through plot intervention.

The bookstore, after a thorough overhaul, was breaking even, my heart was healing, and my soul mate? Let's just say I wasn't completely sold on the idea, but I was intrigued. For his part, well, he had no idea. Tonight's book walk would be the first time I'd see him since he'd realized he wasn't dreaming all of our weird, Victorian-era encounters. I had some explaining to do.

"Babe, basketball," Peter said to Bobbie, as if that was enough to redeem the book I'd chosen. He turned to me. "Penny, I for one, am stoked. Every book should have basketball. Tripp will be cool with it."

Tripp was my soul mate, supposedly, if you believed in that sort of thing, or in gypsy curses. The gypsy magic was a given, seeing as how I'd recently found myself and my friends running around in the plot of a badly written English penny publication from the nineteenth century. There was no rationalizing that away. If I believed in one, I was forced to give the other serious consideration.

At this point, I knew nothing about Tripp, other than his first name and his sexy protective instinct. His character in the last book, *The Murderous Margrave*, was a lieutenant with longish blond hair and the flouncy clothes men wore at the time. Not that my stiff, trussed-up outfits were any better. He thought he was the lieutenant right up until the end of the book when he self-realized in the middle of some high drama, not understanding it wasn't real.

So tonight, I had to explain about the legacy, break the news about the soul mate possibility, and let him know what he was in for next. Bobbie could complain about the book I chose all she wanted, but I needed at least one thing in this whole scenario that was uncomplicated. *Pom Squad* fit the bill.

"Thank you for your support, Peter. Bobbie, I'll let you choose the next book, if we end up needing one. Promise." I patted her knee.

"Okay, Penn. We're ready when you are." Bobbie plastered a fake smile on her face.

"Let's do this. Fingers crossed. 'It was the first pre-season basketball game of the school year…' "

Pom Squad Mystery #17

It was the first pre-season basketball game of the school year, and the Weatherford Warriors were playing to win.

Beth Smart was proud of her team and equally proud of her squad. The Lady Warriors cheer team, more commonly known around school as the pom squad, had been practicing their routines for weeks.

"Shoot for two! Let's win! Hey! We want two!" they shouted in unison.

The Warriors were facing off tonight against the Rams, the team from neighboring town, Fort Duncan.

Steve, Beth's boyfriend and the Warriors' team captain, was at the top of his game. She watched as he dribbled up the court and passed the ball at the last minute to his friend, Roger, who went in for a lay-up shot. The shot was good and the crowd went wild. Steve and Roger high-fived and headed back down the court to take defensive positions.

"Oh no!" another squad member exclaimed. "The other team has the ball! We need to do another cheer."

"Um, er, you go ahead there, ah, friend," Penny said, causing the other girl (Patty?) to beam with pride. She turned to face the court and took the start position.

"READY? O.K.," Patty yelled and the rest of the squad followed her lead. "P, OSS, ESS, ION. We want possession, possession again! Woo hoo! Yah!"

Penny did her best to follow the other girls' movements, thankful that even if anyone noticed, they weren't scripted to say anything about it. She heard a sharp gasp behind her and pivoted to see her best friend Bobbie, attempting to stifle a laugh.

"What's so funny?" I hissed.

"Oh my goodness, Penny…" She took several deep breaths in an effort to control herself. "Look!" She pointed toward the court.

I watched the boys closely. At first glance, nothing stood out as unusual or laughable. I saw a bunch of pasty-white teenage boys with crew cuts. Half were wearing blue and yellow uniforms and half were in red and white, like me, I noticed, so I focused on them.

One boy was less pasty than the others, he was also a bit taller and his arm muscles were better defined. When he turned to intercept a pass, my stomach flopped over, it was Tripp. His hair was much shorter than when I last saw him; I had to stifle my own laugh. I turned back to Bobbie.

"Look, it's Tripp." I pointed.

She grabbed my arm and adjusted the direction so I was pointing at an even taller boy who was actually paler than the others. "And Peter!" She doubled over then and let loose with peals of laughter. My eyes widened and I started chuckling as well. Gone were Peter's shaggy, blond locks, he now sported a buzz cut so short, he appeared to be bald.

"I didn't even know he had a forehead," I whispered to Bobbie. Now that I could really see Peter's face, I had to admit he was more handsome than I'd realized.

The girls started another cheer. Bobbie didn't even bother trying to join them, so I didn't either. She had stopped laughing and was engrossed in watching the court action.

"Steve, or rather, Tripp, is the team captain and Peter is Roger, his best friend and my character's boyfriend. That's why they have the ball most of the time; they are main characters," Bobbie explained.

4

"And you're Sandy, my best friend." Parts of the late-fifties-era mystery series that I'd loved as a pre-teen were coming back to me. I hadn't read a *Pom Squad Mystery* in fifteen years, so I was glad Bobbie was pre-reading again for me, though she informed me it was terribly dull.

The players streaked back to the end of the court, Tripp's face set in a determined frown. He glanced at me and grinned, then his smile faltered, and he slowed almost to a stop, his hand unconsciously still dribbling the ball.

I smiled back at him and offered a little wave. He came to a full stop and held on to the ball. I watched as Peter rushed over and broke our line of sight. I don't know what Peter said to him, but seconds later they were back in the game and quickly dominating the court.

They ran circles around the Rams and their own team mates as well. They played aggressively, and when the refs didn't make any calls, because they weren't scripted, Peter and Tripp got downright rough. They were essentially playing street ball and loving every minute of it if their facial expressions were any indication.

The scoreboard numbers and the crowd's cheers didn't match anything that had happened on the court. As close as I could guess, when the game was over, the score was Warriors 32, Rams 30, Peter and Tripp 106.

The teams headed to the locker room, high-fiving and back-slapping. The cheer team clustered around me.

"What a swell game!" one girl exclaimed.

"Sylvia," Bobbie supplied her name to me in a whisper.

"Oh, yes! Did you see my Alfie score the winning points?" another girl said.

"Linda," Bobbie provided.

I didn't remember seeing any such thing, but I smiled at her anyway. After the four of us arrived in the scene, Peter and Tripp scored all the points, but there was no reason to make an issue of it.

"It's because we were cheering them on; I just know it!" The girl who spoke punched a fist in the air.

"You're right, Patty," Bobbie cut in. "Why, we're almost as important as the players themselves."

My eyes widened at the statement and Bobbie's sugary-sweet tone. I'd never known acting to be her thing, but she was almost believable. Well, 1950's believable in any case.

"Everybody in!" Bobbie yelled, thrusting her hand into the middle of our group. The girls quickly followed suit and I added my own to the top as they all screamed, "1, 2, 3, Go Warriors!" and broke apart with more yells and cheers. As the team dispersed, Bobbie grabbed my hand and pulled me toward the exit.

"Come on. The guys are meeting us out front and we're going to the Malt Shop where we can talk."

"In this?" I looked down at the big, fuzzy, red '*W*' on the front of my white sweater and my calf-length pleated uniform skirt.

She shrugged. "Sure, why not?"

I glanced down at my red and white saddle shoes. It's not like I had anything to change into anyway. "Never mind. Let's go."

Chapter 2

Situational Déjà vu

Pom Squad Mystery #17
Steve tried to clear his mind. The most important thing right now was the game, even if it was only preseason. That wasn't any excuse not to give his best effort. He blocked out the distractions one by one; the crowd cheering, the cheerleaders, led by his girlfriend, Beth, the threatening looks from the Rams players, the sensation of his feet pounding up the court.

He intercepted a Rams pass and headed back up the court, tracking his buddy, Roger, as he ran. He feinted right, then made a quick pass to Roger, who was ready and waiting for it. They made an unstoppable team. Roger made a lay-up shot, then the Warriors moved back to defense positions.

This time, Roger didn't even wait to make an interception. He stole the ball right out of the Ram center's hands and tried to take it back up the court. Rams surrounded him, but Steve was open and ready to catch the pass. Steve's path was clear. With a burst of speed he headed for the basket. Nothing could stop him.

He spared a glance at the pom squad on the sidelines. Was Beth watching him play the hero? He hoped so. Maybe she would reward him with a kiss later.

She was watching him all right, but she wasn't cheering. Beth's long blonde hair…no, that's not right. Beth's auburn curls…no. Penelope's auburn curls fell softly on her shoulders and bounced when she turned to talk to Roger's girl, Sandy.

Why weren't they cheering? This seemed strange to Steve. There didn't appear to be any emergency. His pace slowed. Usually Penelope was his biggest fan. She turned back around and caught his eye. She gave him a little wave, and Tripp stopped completely.

Penelope.

I'm Tripp, not Steve.

Suddenly there was a guy in my face.

"Dude, snap out of it. You know this game, right?" he asked.

I gave him a slight nod while my brain tried to catch up.

"Cool. Then just play and we'll talk after. These boys are no competition. I'm getting bored."

He relieved me of the ball and shot a clean three-pointer. I looked around at the other players. Roger and I were clearly six to ten years older, and adult enough that the uniform shorts we wore were borderline indecent. These kids all looked like they were headed off to basic training. I ran my hand through my own hair. Crap, me too, and I knew it wasn't an attractive look on me. I glanced over at Penelope.

She and her friend watched me nervously. She was here now, and I could only trust she'd be here later to talk, like Roger said. I certainly had questions. So many questions. For now, I wasn't going to pass up the opportunity to play ball. No way in hell.

****

At the buzzer, the crowd and team went wild. Roger and I were lifted onto shoulders and carried off to the locker room. After putting us down, the other players faded quietly to other parts of the locker room, leaving Roger and me basically alone. It was weird. I'd expected more towel-snapping and the other usual teenage boy antics.

"It's because we're the only ones scripted here," Roger said, adding to my confusion. He sighed. "Listen, Penny will explain everything. Get showered so we can leave. And call me Peter." He stuck out his hand.

"Thanks, Peter. Good game out there." I shook his hand.

He grinned wide. "You too, we'll have to pick up a game on the outside. A group of us play on the weekends."

I forced a grin. "Sure, sounds good. Call me Tripp."

The locker room was eerily silent. The only sounds were showers and the occasional slamming locker door. In Steve's locker I found creased khakis and a plaid dress shirt hung neatly on a hanger, a heavy wool letterman's jacket, and…were those penny loafers? I grabbed the leather toiletries kit and a folded towel and headed for the shower.

I was anxious for some answers, anxious to see Penelope. Peter called her Penny. It suited her. Her friend called her Pen the last time we met. I liked that too. It was less formal, and she didn't strike me as a formal sort of girl. I grinned in earnest.

I thought back to the last time I saw her—that amazing kiss. I remembered my heart stopping when she went over the side of the tower wall. Since then, I'd gone over every possible and impossible scenario I could think of to explain what had happened to me. I considered time travel, parallel universe, and alien abduction, but nothing really fit.

I'd decided if it happened again, I'd be alert and prepared, but not sweat the details. Penny and her friend hadn't seemed scared or stressed, so I'd remain calm as well and just take things as they came.

The clothes provided for me, while in the style the others were wearing, seemed to fit my adult body just fine. They were a bit snug in places I wasn't used to, but that was due to the cut rather than the size. I noticed Peter's clothes had a similar slim fit.

"Ready to go?" He slapped me on the back.

"Where?" I followed him out of the locker room. The gymnasium lights were off and the bleachers empty.

"We're supposed to meet the girls at the Malt Shop."

"Malt?"

"Yeah, like a milkshake."

"I know, I just don't hear that term very often, or ever."

"Well, it's like 1960 here, dude, so just roll with it."

We left through the gymnasium doors. It was warm enough to not need my jacket, but not so warm that I needed to remove it. I estimated the season to be early to mid-fall, depending on what part of the country we were in. Peter looked around, then headed left, toward what appeared to be the main street.

Though I wasn't much of a car guy, I couldn't help but appreciate all the vintage automobiles lining the street. It felt like some kind of ghost-town car show.

Peter whistled. "Man, what I wouldn't give for one of these." He pointed at a powder blue convertible.

"Cherry condition like that, sweet! I'd love to take it back with me."

"Back?"

"Sort of. I can't really explain it. Penny will, though, not that it will make it seem any more believable. I'm just along for the ride."

"Just roll with it, right?"

"Exaaactly." He smiled.

We arrived at the malt shop, literally named 'The Malt Shop.' Through the window, I could see the girls seated inside, still in their uniforms. I didn't know Penny very well, but I could tell she was nervous. All the booths seemed to be filled with high school students, fresh from the game.

A bell tinkled as we entered, and the smell of greasy burgers enveloped me. Cheers and shouts greeted us as we made our way to the girls' table in the back. Peter slid into the booth next to Penny's friend and gave her a kiss that seemed way more PG-13 than this G-rated world we seemed to be stuck in. I took the last available spot next to Penny.

"Hey." Really? That's the best I could do?

"Tripp." She appeared to be as lost for words as I was. Surprising, considering the circumstances. I had a lot of questions, and she, hopefully, had a lot of answers.

Peter finished greeting Penny's friend, obviously his girlfriend, and she turned her attention to me.

"Hi! I'm Bobbie, Penny's best friend. We sort of met once before, but you might not remember. Here, I'm Sandy, Roger's girlfriend."

"I'm unlikely to ever forget the last time we met." I turned to look Penny directly in the eyes. She gave me a half-smile.

"Yes, well, I'm sure you have tons of questions and Penny"—she gave her friend a pointed look—"is excited to answer them for you."

The girl sitting next to me looked anything but excited. I angled my body and turned my full attention on her. My heart lightened and I smiled. I don't know what it was about her in particular. She wasn't the prettiest girl I'd ever seen, but top ten certainly. There was something else I couldn't pinpoint that drew me. I should be freaking out about this crazy situation and demanding answers. Instead, I sat there with an idiot grin on my face. I released a breath when she smiled back. Whatever it was, she felt it too. I just hoped maybe she could explain it. I thought back to that kiss from the last time we met, and my body instinctively swayed toward her.

"Ahem." Bobbie cleared her throat. "You don't really have time for that."

Penny blinked her amazing hazel eyes, breaking the spell, and leaned against the back of our seat.

"So, Tripp," she started. "I'm Penny, as you know from last time, and we're here because my family has a gypsy curse on it."

"Legacy." Bobbie pointed a finger at her friend and frowned.

That possibility never even occurred to me. Out of all the unbelievable options, it was an obscure one.

"Anyway," she continued, "it's a thing with the women in my family that I have no control over, and you're here because the universe has designated you as my soul mate."

This all came out in a rush, and she gave me an embarrassed, yet apologetic look. Oh yeah, she knew exactly how crazy she sounded. But isn't recognizing the crazy a sign you weren't actually crazy? I'd heard enough psychobabble recently to allow that it might be the case.

"We'll get back to the soul mate part later. What I really want to know is, where is here and why is it a different here than the last time I saw you?"

"That's a little harder to explain." She winced. I knew I wouldn't like what was coming. "We're actually inside the plot of a book. The reason it's different than last time is because I finished reading that book, *The Murderous Margrave*. It was my first time and kind of a surprise, so this time I tried to pick a book with a little less drama…and less old."

"It isn't possible to be inside a written work of fiction. I'd be more apt to believe in some kind of telepathic group psychosis."

"Yet, here we are." She raised her brows.

A middle-aged woman in a light blue dress and little white apron stepped over to our table.

"I heard it was a great game tonight, guys. Sorry I missed it." She paused, as if waiting for a response, but before I could formulate the right words, she continued. "You can say that again! What will it be tonight?"

"The usual, please," Bobbie said.

"Coming right up," the waitress said and hurried back to the kitchen.

"There'll be some more dialogue when she comes back. You don't have to respond, I think she'll just keep going anyway," Bobbie explained.

I turned back to Penny. "OK, say we're in a book. How did we get here and what book is it?"

13

"It's *Pom Squad Mystery #17*. It's kind of like a Nancy Drew mystery or Hardy Boys. Based on what I've learned about the legacy, when I read a book, I, and anyone nearby, are transported into it. We just kind of find ourselves there in the plot as main characters. You are here, like I said, because you are supposedly my soul mate." She cringed again.

Was she cringing because of the situation or because she didn't think I'd make a decent soul mate? What was I even thinking? I wasn't in the market for a soul mate, especially one I didn't even pick myself. The thought of Penny not thinking I was good enough still rankled, though. I was being ridiculous.

"Okay. So, let's say I am your soul mate. What's supposed to happen? And what's happening to my body when my mind is here? I assume my body is still where I left it since I haven't been reported missing."

"Oh, don't worry, no time passes on the outside while you're here." She put her hand on my arm, then quickly removed it.

"And the end game?"

She blushed; it looked good on her.

"I'm supposed to get you to self-realize, that is, realize you aren't actually the character you're portraying, then figure out how to meet in real life, then live happily ever after, I guess?"

"You guess?"

She twisted her hands together nervously in her lap. "Well, that's what my grandmothers said happened to them in the letters they wrote about the legacy. This was a very unexpected turn of events, I promise you. I was not in the market for a husband when I accidently read into *Margrave*."

14

"That guy…"

"The last book was an old Victorian penny publication. How much do you remember?"

"I remember the last part really well." She blushed again. I would never get tired of making her do that. "I remember that terrorist guy you killed. I remember clothes and horses and bits and pieces of meeting you. Rescuing you." Our gazes met again. I couldn't remember what I'd been saying.

"Yes, er, there was quite a bit of rescuing in that story."

"Here you go! Usuals all around." Our waitress slid four plates and four drinks onto our table. She leaned in and whispered, "I upgraded those shakes to larges for our star players, on the house."

"Thank you, Flo!" Bobbie said.

"Is the team ready for homecoming? It's only two weeks away." She paused. "I think so too. The whole town is excited for the dance and pep rally. It's not every year we get to look into the past. You know, I was in high school myself when the time capsule was filled. The student council asked for something significant from each of the four high school grade levels, but I can't for the life of me remember what any of the items were." Pause. "Ha, ha. It sure will be a better surprise that way. You kids enjoy your meals." At that, she walked off and disappeared through the swinging door to the kitchen.

I looked at Penny. "What was all that about?"

She looked across the table at Bobbie to supply an answer.

"It's part of the plot. Our characters are supposed to be having a conversation about the time capsule and homecoming," she explained.

"Bobbie reads ahead in the books for me so I know what to expect." Penny shrugged. "Whenever I read them, I end up in them, so we decided to pre-read as a safety precaution. Especially in light of some of the surprises in the last book."

"It's not really foolproof though, is it?" I asked.

"There's a learning curve," she admitted. "That's why we picked something nice and safe this time."

"*Pom Squad Mystery*? I've never heard of it?" I dug into my fries. They were surprisingly good for being fictional.

"It's pretty old. Nineteen fifties or sixties, in case you couldn't tell. And marketed toward girls, I wouldn't expect you to have heard of it."

"Is this going to happen to us whenever you read a book for the rest of our lives?"

"Well, no." She brought her straw to her lips.

I raised my eyebrows at her. I didn't think she could turn any deeper red, but I was wrong.

She swallowed. "As soon as I'm wearing my grandmother's wedding band in marriage, everything will go back to normal."

"To me?" Marriage. As in, to my real self, in the real world? My fry lodged in my throat, then continued down in a solid lump.

"Not necessarily. I think the curse, I mean legacy, would respect marriage vows. That's how this all got started, after all. My way-back great-grandmother married someone who wasn't her soul mate, so the magic passed to her granddaughter."

"And are you in a hurry for that to happen?" I searched her gaze.

"Oh no! Not at all. I'm not ready to get married. I totally started on this legacy thing by accident. But then I met you, and, well, I didn't think there was any harm in getting to know you better. I'm sorry. I should have stopped after the first book, but you'd self-realized, and I knew you'd have questions, so…" Her eyes begged me to understand her unfathomable situation. Oddly enough, I did. Not the legacy part; I foresaw some serious gypsy research in my future, but it sounded like she was just as drawn to me as I to her. That made me feel better about my crazy gut reactions to someone I didn't even know.

"Our time's almost up." Bobbie pointed to the clock behind the counter. "Curfew is in twenty minutes, and Beth's dad will be here to pick her up."

"OK, Tripp, here's the thing. I need to know if you're good with this." She waved her hand in the air, I guess to indicate the crazy that was now our lives. "Cause if you're not, if I'm disrupting your life too much, I'll just stop. I won't pick the book up again. According to the grandmother letters, we would eventually meet each other in some natural way anyhow. This just magically speeds up the process. But I'll stop if you want."

Did I want? I'd only start looking for her around every corner. I'd dream about her eyes and the scent of her hair. I think I'd prefer to meet my crazy head-on rather than have it mess with my mind. I could delude myself that I was in some kind of control.

"No. Don't stop reading. We're not in any hurry. We can get to know each other here just as easily as in real life. We'll have all these really interesting free dates without having to leave home." Did I really just say that? She's going to think I'm cheap now and lazy. I have

17

absolutely no game tonight, at least off the court. I caught Peter smirking at me and frowned.

Penny sighed in relief. "That sounds perfect." And finally, she leaned over and kissed me.

Chapter 3

Back to Life, Back to Reality

I would never get used to the phenomenon of returning from an hours-long book sojourn to find my coffee still piping hot. I took a grateful sip, peering over the mug's rim as Bobbie did the same and Peter adjusted to being back. This was his second book trip with us and his first on-purpose visit.

"How you doing, babe?" Bobbie reached over to grasp his hand.

"I'm good. That was fun. Tripp seems cool; he didn't totally flip out, at least."

"He didn't freeze-up either," Bobbie noted, referring to the time my sort-of neighbor, Gregorio, ended up with us in *Margrave*.

"I can't imagine what he must be thinking, though, probably that I'm some kind of contagious lunatic."

"More likely, that he's gone round the bend himself." Peter stood and stretched as if he'd just played in a real game.

"Thank you, guys, for going with me." I looked at Peter. "I know you were really integral when Tripp self-realized in the middle of the game."

"No problem. I'm totally up for anymore basketball read-ins."

"Bobbie will have to let you know. She's my puppet master." I smiled in her direction. I was so lucky to have her as my best friend; not only was she super-smart, but she dealt really well with all of my crazy. And she'd made it her mission to untangle all the unwritten rules of how my family legacy worked. We'd already learned quite a bit and it allowed me to have at least some control over my encounters with Tripp.

I, on the other hand, was somewhat of a slacker. My job was to try to see how or if the legacy's magic could be broken. One of my grandmothers theorized that when one of her descendants finally hooked up with a descendent of the original "true love," the magic would be fulfilled and the curse cease.

The problem was figuring out who that could have been. Fortunately, we had a few clues. Elizabeth, the many-great-grandmother who started it all, mentions three men who "might have been," and I've been trying to track them down. Unfortunately, she only referred to them by occupation, rather than by name, making it a bit challenging. After the first dead-end, I put off starting the process again with bachelor number two.

Of course, it might not have been any of those three and this will prove to be a wild goose chase. But the evidence suggests that her true love was someone she would have met anyway during the normal course of her life, so I'm optimistic.

It would be cool if Tripp turned out to be the descendent and I'm the one to end the curse, but since I'm the fifth granddaughter afflicted, I'm not holding my breath. So, Bobbie has been taking careful notes on how the legacy works for my granddaughter. My and Tripp's granddaughter. The thought gave me weird, not unpleasant, shivers.

My contribution would be all the descendent information available, so that future generations would be able to update it as needed. It won't really make a difference. We won't be able to force the curse to end, but maybe my granddaughter will find some comfort in having as much information as possible. And I'll sure as heck tell her all about it so she won't be surprised when I'm dead.

"When do you want to get together again?" I pulled up the calendar on my phone.

Bobbie was working toward her master's degree, so wasn't always available during the week. Reading-in didn't take any time, really, since we always returned the same moment we left. But afterward, the note taking and rehashing of what we learned took a little bit. It was also overwhelming for me emotionally, so I usually needed to process and decompress.

"The next scene takes place at school when the mystery presents itself. You can do it on your own if you want, I'm not in those scenes. Beth gathers information, but it mostly comes to her, she doesn't have to go seek it out. You'll get info on the time capsule and be introduced to some of the key characters." Bobbie flipped through the yellowing pages of *Pom Squad*.

"Will Tripp be there?"

"Yes, you meet him in the library, the scene of the crime, during study period."

"Maybe later tonight then. I don't feel like I'm explaining things very well."

"You did fine. It's a lot for anyone to absorb." She handed me the book.

"So, is tonight too soon?" I pulled my hand back.

Bobbie considered me for a moment. "You both agreed there wasn't any hurry. Why don't you wait till later in the week. Don't look too eager."

"You're right. I guess that leaves me with the rest of the day to dig back into the research side of things." I groaned internally.

Bobbie put the book on the coffee table. "Who's next? The store owner?"

"Yep."

"Good luck," She turned to Peter. "Ready to go?"

"Whenever you are." He released his hamstring and took Bobbie's bag.

"Bye, guys, thanks again."

Bobbie gave me a quick hug as she and Peter departed. "Anytime. I'm having fun with it."

I locked the shop door behind them and headed upstairs to my apartment. I collected all my previous notes and my laptop and set up my workspace at the kitchen table. It made me feel like a more serious researcher than my normal spot on the couch.

Joseph Cleary was listed in the church count paperwork from 1735. The church rep who took the count was also a potential true-love bachelor, but I had eliminated him due to his temporary status in the community, the likelihood of his being a candidate for Catholic priesthood, and because I couldn't find his name on any of the documents. If I'm being honest, it was mostly the last reason. I may have to circle back to him if the other two don't pan out, but for now, I focused on the easier options.

As a store owner, Cleary, would have plenty of opportunity to interact with Elizabeth. I needed to find out if he ever married and trace his descendants as far as I could. I really hoped his line was as sparse as my own, because if he fathered ten kids, I was in trouble.

Since I'd already found the church census from 1735, it was easy to find the subsequent Westmeath counts; they did them every five to seven years.

Mr. Cleary married Anna and they'd had two boys by 1735 and two more children, girls, by 1740. The 1745 count showed two boys and one girl, but the ages were off. I surmised that they must have lost a boy and girl but had another boy. I'd have to look at birth and death records to confirm this, though. This poor family, long dead, that I didn't even know, saddened me. I said a short prayer of thanks for the miracle of modern medicine.

Having to track down three kids wouldn't be so bad. My eyes were crossing on their own from staring at the antiquated documents and my spirits took a nosedive. That was enough for one day.

After working and snacking through lunch, the clock read almost three thirty when I called it quits. I considered again reading back in after an early dinner, but decided boredom drove me rather than desire to make progress in my relationship with Tripp. Instead, I heated a frozen pizza and binge watched a sci-fi series until a reasonable bedtime.

Chapter 4

The Boy Next Door

An industrial dumpster greeted me in the back alley when I took the trash out Wednesday morning. I hoped this meant Gregorio was getting ready to start remodeling the shop next door and not that someone had misplaced a giant dumpster. My suspicions were confirmed later that morning when demolition sounds began filtering through our shared wall.

Gregorio had cleared most of the stock from his late uncle's shop. I'm not sure where the tobacco products ended up, but many of the nicer leather goods were consigned to me. Some days I sold more leather than I did books.

Gregorio planned to remodel the shop and overhead apartment in a more neutral palette and floor plan, then try to lease or sell it. As a builder and property flipper, he had no real need for a brick and mortar store front. He saved money by living nomadically in his current projects, so he had no use for the upstairs apartment, either.

I was apprehensive about having a new neighbor, but Gregorio assured me he planned to be a discerning landlord and take my preferences into consideration. A generous concession considering I called a halt to our almost-relationship last month. I really would have loved to date him. He was gorgeous, funny, kind, oh, and gorgeous. But when it came right down to decision time, I couldn't ignore the pesky feelings developing for Tripp, as much as I'd would have liked to deny them on principle.

The idea of Tripp having a girlfriend in real life made me uncomfortable in ways I'd rather not explore, so I figured I should probably not date anyone either. If there was no Tripp, I could easily see myself falling for Gregorio. That path would only lead to eventual heartache and the loss of a friend, so just friends we would remain.

At lunch I meandered over to check the reno's progress. The ruckus had fallen silent, so I figured I wouldn't be in the way.

"Hey." I found him sitting on a tub of drywall mud eating a sandwich.

"Penelope, hello!" He cast around for a seat to offer me before deciding to sacrifice his own.

"No, don't get up. I heard you working. You deserve a rest. How's it going?"

Gregorio didn't sit back down. His manners were very old-school, which I loved, but offered to give me a tour of the destruction instead.

"The upstairs didn't need too much work," he explained as we climbed the stairs. "My uncle had updates made before he moved in, after my aunt died."

At the top of the stairs, he opened the door and ushered me into a living room similar to my own, but smelling of fresh paint.

"I left the carpet in the bedroom but ripped out everything else to put in laminate."

"It's really beautiful." I admired how the blond flooring brightened the room. "I might have to hire you to come do mine when you finish here."

"Of course. I'll give you a friends and family discount." He displayed his perfect white teeth.

I briefly lamented turning down his suit as I returned his smile. "Thanks, I'll let you know. The store will have to start making money before I can even consider it."

"This is true," he agreed.

"So," Gregorio asked as we headed back downstairs. "Read any good books lately?"

I glanced back over my shoulder at his fake innocent smile.

"As a matter of fact, I started a mystery book where a clever teen cheerleading captain and her team solve small-town petty crimes."

"Sounds safe. Given up horseback riding, have you?" His eyes danced with mirth.

"For now. I need something a little less action packed." We arrived back in the shop area.

"Sounds tame. I'll try to stay out of your way nonetheless." He winked.

"So, what are your plans down here?"

"I'm not sure yet. I hoped to list it as a potential cafe, but the cost involved to bring it up to code was prohibitive. Whoever rents the space may be able to offer a small coffee bar like you have, but other than that, it will have to be strictly retail or office space."

"How long before you can offer it?" To me, it looked like a long, long time.

"No more than a few weeks," he answered, surprising me.

"Really?" I surveyed the space again.

"A friend of my mother's wants to take a look this weekend. She has a small insurance office and is thinking about selling her house and combining her home and business spaces."

"She would make a quiet neighbor, I imagine."

Gregorio nodded. "Oh yes, Cora is a very sweet lady. She's like an aunt to me."

"Well, I hope it works out." I glanced around the room. This transition from almost-relationship to neighbor and friend was a little unconventional, especially since I still found Gregorio wildly attractive. He seemed to sense my unease.

"So, how is it going with the guy?"

"Oh, you mean Tripp?" I know I'd told him Tripp's name one time when we visited, and I'd filled him in on how *The Murderous Margrave* ended. He had no choice but to believe my unbelievable story since he'd inadvertently found himself a part of it. His supposedly forgetting Tripp's name made me suspect our friendship status made him a little uncomfortable as well.

"Yes, Tripp. Have you learned anymore about him?"

"Not much. I've only seen him once since *Margrave* ended. He took the whole curse business pretty well, I think. He didn't freak out or anything."

He colored slightly. "You mean like I did?"

I smiled. "I think yours were extenuating circumstances. You did self-realize in the middle of a kidnapping and near sexual assault."

He winced. "I'm so sorry about that, Penelope..."

I held up my hand to stop him before he could continue. It happened while he was the evil titular character and stopped the moment he was himself again, but he would not quit beating himself up about it.

"Stop. It wasn't you, so stop. No harm done. You need to get to a place where you can joke about it with me."

"I can't help but feel it has a bearing on our relationship now."

"It absolutely does not. Gregorio, I promise, I would like nothing better than to get involved with you. Trust me. But I actually, sort-of, have a road map to follow in this situation, and I don't want to put either of us in a position to have our hearts broken."

The grandmother letters were pretty clear about how the family legacy was never wrong when it came to true love. I came from a long line of happy couples to prove it. I'm drawn to Tripp in a way that I'm not to Gregorio, even before I even knew his real name.

Both men were insanely attractive, though looked nothing alike, and both had impeccable manners. Gregorio's were real. I still didn't know for sure if Tripp's personality is really his or if much of it was residual from his character in *Margrave*, Lieutenant Culver Eberhart.

"I would have liked to see where a relationship between us would have gone, but I understand, mostly. I just don't want my bad behavior to be between us, even as friends. If you are ready to joke about it, I will try to move past it as well."

"Thank you, but please, stopping claiming that bad behavior as yours. I know it was never you." I reached over to squeeze his hand. "I'd better get back to the shop. Thanks for the tour."

"Anytime. Have a good afternoon, Penelope."

No customers waited for me when I returned to the book shop; no surprise there, so I settled in for a boring afternoon. I brought my laptop downstairs with me, anticipating a slow day in which to do some more research. Banging sounds next door soon accompanied my keyboard pecking.

It had been a lot easier following my family tree backward than following Joseph Cleary's forward. I suppose, because I knew where and when I'd end up in the past. When searching forward, you know a person left when they are simply not found in the next census record. Then you have to find out if they're gone or dead. Unpleasant business, that.

The oldest boy, Gerald, disappeared from records in 1755, and the girl, Virginia, in 1760. Luckily, a Virginia with the right age showed up that same year with a different last name. I wished they were all so easy.

The youngest son, Geoffrey, remained with the family and eventually added a wife. I assume he was the good son who took over the family business. His name remained with the household even after old Joseph died. But where did Gerald go?

Following every branch would get hairy. Stalwart Ginny had twelve kids, and Geoff and his wife, seven.

Pursuing the missing Gerald seemed less daunting, by comparison, but where would I start? He could be almost anywhere—England, the US, even Australia. He disappeared between 1750 and 1755. I guess I should start with death records first, as well as marriages. He might have simply married and moved to another parish with his wife.

Another time-saving search strategy I considered was following a similar pattern to that of my own family.

The legacy was passed to the first daughter of every other generation after Sarah. Would a similar pattern exist on the male side? That would be awesome, but even so, still left me with the Gerald problem.

I glanced around the shop. No customers made for a slow afternoon. It was already closing time. Thank goodness. I could put Gerald off for another day. Maybe a brilliant search avenue would occur to me in the next couple days. Best to give it a rest for now.

Chapter 5

It's Complicated

I managed to hold off until Friday night before succumbing to my eagerness and picking up *Pom Squad Mystery #17* again. Bobbie and Peter were on a date, but I didn't need them for this section. Tripp would be expecting me, sort of; at least he wouldn't be surprised and confused.

I settled in to the couch, my favorite read-in spot, with a steaming mug of chamomile, ready for me when I came back. I'd undoubtedly need its calming effects to help me sleep afterward.

Pom Squad Mystery #17
The morning after the big game Beth and Steve made plans to meet in the library during study hall. Beth was a science whiz and usually helped Steve with his lab work. In return, Steve helped Beth with her math. She didn't really need his assistance, but she wanted him to feel like things were even.

She chose a quiet table near the card catalogs, straightened her collar, and pinched her cheeks for color while she waited. Steve arrived momentarily, dumping his books on the table.

"Sorry I'm late," Steve said. "My dad asked me to fill him in on the game last night since he couldn't attend." Steve's dad was the mayor and his important job often kept him from attending school events.

"I just arrived myself," Beth said. "I can tell you were in a hurry." She laughed. "Your jacket is misbuttoned."

Steve looked down at his red wool letterman's jacket and, indeed, one button hung free without a buttonhole to match. He blushed as red as his coat and quickly unbuttoned it all the way. He slipped it off, revealing a crisp blue plaid button-up that complemented his eyes. He draped the jacket over the back of the chair and sat down next to Beth.

"I already finished my lab work, but I wanted to spend time with you anyway."

"That's sweet," Beth said. "I don't have any math today either. What shall we talk about?"

"SHHH!" Ms. Frank, the librarian, shushed them from where she was shelving books nearby.

Beth pulled a book from her satchel at random and opened it on the table.

Steve quietly cleared his throat. "I hoped to talk to you about the homecoming dance coming up next week."

"Oh, yes! The squad and I are jazzed. We've been asked to serve as the steering committee, you know?" Beth's face glowed with excitement.

"That's great news," Steve said. "I know you girls will do a terrific job." He hesitated. "I was wondering if you had a plan yet for the dance itself."

"We haven't made a plan yet. Principal Dunn just approached me about it this morning. I'm sure someone will need to be in charge of decorations and someone else for refreshments. We'll need someone who will be good at playing records, or do you think there's enough time to find a band?" Beth made a list in neat, precise handwriting as she spoke.

Tripp sighed, once Penny got started planning something, it was difficult to get her to talk about anything else.

"Penny." Tripp reached over and touched my hand. I blinked away my plans for tissue paper flowers and cookies frosted with school colors.

"Tripp!" I smiled at him.

"So, what are the rules?" His warm hand covered mine.

"The rules?" My brain fog slowly cleared.

"To your crazy family curse."

I bristled slightly and he back-pedaled.

"Not that your family is crazy, but that these circumstances are well outside the norm."

I rolled my eyes. "Thanks for clarifying. I don't know all the rules, per se. Bobbie and I have discovered a few things and the grandmother letters explained quite a bit, too."

"What are the grandmother letters? You mentioned them last time."

I opened my mouth to respond, but Tripp interrupted.

"Hold on. What I want to know first, is do we have to stay here or can we go somewhere else?"

"We have to be here for the plot to move forward, which should happen any time. At the end of the scene, we'll wake up." I made air quotes with my fingers. "On the outside."

"So what if we leave before the scene is finished? Will we be able to stay longer, then come back and finish later? I want to talk without weird interruptions, like the waitress the other night." He was already pushing his chair back and shrugging his jacket back on.

"We can try. If we get kicked out of the story, I can just read us back in." I stood and put on my sweater.

"Great!" Tripp grabbed my hand and dragged me stumbling out of the library. In the hallway, he spotted a stairwell to the right. It took us downstairs to the main hall. The cafeteria was on the left, directly across from the main entrance. The building was eerily quiet and there were no other students in the hall. The front office was similarly deserted. We could have gone anywhere in the school and been alone; I said as much to Tripp.

"Well, I didn't know that rule, now did I? Anyway, I don't like being closed up in unfamiliar places." He headed for the exit.

Outside, a beautiful, Indian summer day greeted us. The trees across the parking lot were turning and the air smelled like autumn. It really messed with my senses. Home was in the middle of a rainy mid-May. Tripp still held my hand and pulled me to sit on a bench along a path leading to the athletic fields.

"So, where are all the people?" His eyes never stopped scanning our surroundings. Not in a paranoid way, but Tripp appeared to be a man rarely caught by surprise.

"This isn't like another world where people are living their lives. The only characters present are the ones in this scene, back in the library, and us," I explained.

"How far could we go before we walked out of the book? Could we steal a car and drive to Vegas?"

"I don't know. Sometimes the magic takes measures to keep me in check," I said, remembering Bobbie's attempt in *Margrave* to help me avoid a particularly unpleasant scene. "For instance, it won't let me start reading in the middle of a scene, it will kick me back to the beginning. If we tried to depart from the scene entirely, I'm pretty sure it would kick us out of the book or back to the library."

"That's a good rule to know. I wonder how long it will let us stay here?"

"A while, I imagine, as long as our intentions are good."

Tripp gave me a questioning look.

"As long as we are trying to get to know each other. I think if we were fighting or plotting to break the spell, it might kick us out."

"Isn't that the whole point? To find true love." He grimaced. "And break the curse?"

"No," I corrected. "We aren't breaking the curse; we're trying to satisfy the magic." I fidgeted in my seat.

Tripp leaned forward and rested his elbows on his knees. "This is the most insane relationship I've ever been in."

"Is it? I mean, are you?" I let out an exasperated sigh. "Are you in a relationship? I mean, you don't have a girlfriend or wife or something back in your real life, do you?" I asked, though I was pretty sure the magic wouldn't have worked if he had been married. It did seem to have some ethical standards, at least.

"No," he said shortly. "I'm single. But as attracted to you as I am, I don't want to define our relationship until we know each other better."

"Aw, and here I was hoping you were ready to put a ring on it." I wiggled my left hand in the air.

Without smiling, he cut his gaze to me. "You were going to explain the grandmother letters."

Apparently, the subject of our relationship status remained firmly closed for now. I don't know why his arbitrary stance on the subject irritated me so much. I wholeheartedly agreed. But he was coming off as the grand final decision maker in our non-relationship, and that didn't sit well. "Actually, I was going to suggest getting to know each other before pursuing a relationship. How do I even know you're not a criminal or something?"

Tripp ground his teeth together. Score one for me. "I guess that's just a chance you're going to have to take."

Infuriating male! I moved on. "The grandmother letters are exactly that. Each of my great-grandmothers who were afflicted with the legacy wrote a letter, explaining the process to the best of their knowledge and adding any new rules they discovered."

"How long has this been going on?"

"Elizabeth, the originator, bought the gypsy magic around 1732. Then her granddaughter, and every other generation after that."

Tripp whistled faintly through his teeth. "Geez. So, have you always been this way?"

"No. The legacy doesn't transfer until the one who holds it dies. My gram passed away six months ago. That's when it passed to me."

"You haven't read anything in six months?"

His condescending tone offended me a little, so I ignored it. "Another rule, which my gram discovered, is that it doesn't work with e-books. That's usually what I read. Picking up *Margrave* last month was a total fluke."

"Is that the kind of thing you usually read?"

"Not hardly!" I laughed. "Gram also left me her used bookstore. Bobbie and I were taking inventory when I started reading it as a joke."

"Looks like the joke was on you." He smiled and I got a peek at the dimple on his cheek.

I quirked an eyebrow at the blatant cliché. "On us, actually."

"Touché." His grin deepened.

"So how do you suggest we get to know each other?" I rose from the bench. I needed to move while I thought. "Just exchange laundry lists of likes and dislikes?"

"No." Tripp leaned back on the bench and watched me pace. "There's no need to rush, is there?"

I stopped and met his gaze. "No, I'm not in any hurry."

He nodded. "Okay, then there isn't any reason we shouldn't proceed as we would in a normal relationship. If we just spend time together, things should evolve naturally."

I had resumed pacing but stopped again. "Normal? Naturally? How shall we accomplish that, pray tell?"

"Well, every time we end up here is like a date, right? And there's plenty to do...you like basketball, right?"

"We can't get to know each other with you playing and me on the sidelines." I frowned.

"Just checking. Getting to know each other already, see?" He gave me an innocent look.

"I like basketball just fine, though I'm not big on any particular sport," I answered honestly, hoping he wasn't some sort of face-painting, tailgating fanatic. "What about you?"

"I used to play basketball and softball recreationally, so playing with Peter the other day was a real blast." A shadow dropped over his face. "I don't get much time for it anymore. I'm mostly an armchair quarterback now."

I pushed forward, in an attempt to dispel Tripp's sudden funk. "So, other than hanging out after ball games, what did you have in mind?"

He surveyed the school campus. "Have you ever thought about reading something that takes place in Hawaii or California?"

"Maybe next time. We're stuck here till the story plays out. Sorry."

"Right. What's the name of this book again?"

"Pom Squad Mystery #17"

"So how about we solve the mystery?"

"Huh?"

"You said we're stuck here anyway, so we can get to know each other. We can exchange facts about ourselves all day long, but I think working together on a project is a better way. Even if it is a dorky teen girl mystery."

I considered Tripp's idea. It wasn't a bad one, actually. "Bobbie usually reads ahead to let me know what to expect."

"That's fine. She can still warn you about possible threats, but she doesn't need to give away the plot."

"I suppose not. You don't think it will be too juvenile for us?"

"It may be, but honestly, I could use a little juvenile in my life right now." Tripp's serious expression belied the levity of his words. I wondered what his real life was like.

I returned to the bench and put my hand on his knee. "I'm sorry. Do you want to talk about it?"

"No, it's nothing. I own my own business, so it gets a little overwhelming at times."

"Really? What kind of business?"

He shrugged. "Sporting goods, mostly."

I didn't press for more despite his vague answer. "Ah, that would explain your interest in basketball."

"Sure," he replied, shrugging again and forcing a smile. "If we're going to solve this mystery, we'd better head back to the library." He stood and offered me his hand. I took it and we walked back to the school together.

Chapter 6

Dum, Da Dum, Dum Dum

Pom Squad Mystery #17

Tripp and I had resumed our seats at the library table when a scream sounded from the circulation desk. He was half out of his chair before he stopped and looked at me. "Is this it?"

I had been expecting some sort of drama, so was less startled by the commotion. "I believe so. We need to be on-scene to find clues and search for evidence."

As we approached the desk, I took note of the characters present. Ms. Frank was sprawled in a chair and a student fanned her with an FHA brochure. The elderly library aide was on the phone, calling the office for assistance. Several stereotypically clean-cut students hovered around looking dismayed. Behind the circulation desk sat an empty trophy case with its glass door slid open.

I peeked over the desk. In front of the case, a few chunks of dried mud littered the otherwise impeccable gray carpet. I tugged Tripp's sleeve and pointed out my discovery.

"Great job, Watson," he said with a grin.

"Why do you get to be Holmes? I'm the main character in this story," I whispered.

Principal Dunn burst through the library door, saving him from responding.

"Eloise! What's happened?" He suddenly registered the students' curious looks and no immediate signs of chaos. "Ahem, I mean, Ms. Frank, what seems to be the trouble?"

The librarian roused herself and smiled gratefully at the student fanning her. "Oh, Mr. Dunn! It's just terrible! The time capsule has been stolen! I know you were counting on opening it at homecoming. This is such a travesty!"

"Now, now, Ms. Frank. The most important thing is your safety and the safety of our students. Tell me what happened."

"Well, I was just opening the case to dust, like I do every Thursday. I must have walked by here a dozen times this morning, but it's been here for so long, I don't even notice it anymore. Anyway, when I opened the case, I realized the capsule was no longer resting on its base. I screamed and felt faint."

At this point, everyone turned to look at Tripp and me, so I guessed in the book, I must have asked a question.

Ms. Frank said, "I have a key of course, the office probably has a copy, and Mr. Louie, the custodian has one as well."

"Uh, thanks?" I muttered.

Ms. Frank was speaking again. "Oh no, I'm sure it was there yesterday. On Wednesdays I clean the inside and outside of the glass. It was definitely there then."

Tripp stepped away, then quickly returned, handing me my notebook. "Here you go, Nancy. Better start writing this stuff down."

I made a list of possible suspects: Mr. Dunn, Ms. Frank, Mr. Louie, office staff. Then I noted the window of time in which the crime took place, and the mud on the floor. Tripp nudged my arm and pointed to the principal's shoes, and specifically, the traces of mud on said shoes.

As if answering my unspoken question, Mr. Dunn said, "The sprinkler system sprang a leak sometime last night. I've been helping Mr. Louie get it under control. It's made quite a mess."

I assumed Mr. Louie's shoes would also have mud on them. I noted Ms. Frank's did not. I wandered over to the case. There was a faint layer of dust on the shelves, but none present where the capsule sat, lending support to the time frame of the theft.

"What if it was those awful Cavaliers!?" Ms. Frank exclaimed.

"How would they even get into our school?" asked a girl in a plaid skirt.

"This would be just the kind of awful homecoming prank they would pull," a boy in a letterman's jacket added.

Random muttering ensued. Tripp and I stood there and watched the corny scene unfold. "How much longer?" he asked. "I don't think we're going to get any more information."

Mr. Dunn spoke, "Now let's settle down and not cast out wild accusations. I'll call the campus police. I'm hopeful they will be able to track it down."

I added "Cavaliers" to my suspect list. I clicked my pen closed and tapped it against my lips as I thought.

My knuckle hit my chin, sans pen. I was home.

Chapter 7

Does that make me a *Square*?

"So, you don't want me to read ahead anymore?" Bobbie asked skeptically.

"No, I mean, I do, but just don't tell me about it, unless, you know, my life is going to be in jeopardy."

"And you guys are going to 'date?'" More skepticism.

"We're going to get to know each other by working on a project together. The project being to solve the time capsule mystery."

It was Saturday afternoon and Bobbie was helping me with the steady trickle of customers in the shop, as well as updating our shelf inventory. I filled her in on my last visit to 1950-something, at least the unscripted parts. She was interested to learn we could leave the scene for an undetermined length of time and pick it back up whenever we wanted. She added the information to her thickening legacy-rules notebook.

She rolled her eyes. "Why don't you just find out where he is and meet up in real life?"

"He seems really hesitant to take our relationship to the next level, or any level, actually. So, I didn't ask. This is okay. Actually, it's a time-saver, since we can meet up and not lose any real time."

"Well, that's a glowing endorsement. Hey, honey, I love dating you because I don't have to sacrifice any actual time from my real life."

"That isn't how we're looking at it," I replied hotly.

She shrugged. "Whatever. Sounds like a cop-out to me."

"Tripp didn't ask for any of this. He's dealing with it rather calmly. I don't mind taking our relationship as slow as he wants, especially since I didn't ask for it either."

She stepped over a pile of books on the floor and gave me a hug. "Chill. I'm sorry. You do this however you want, and I'll try to keep my opinions to myself. You know that everyone in a blissfully happy relationship thinks everyone else's lives would be better if they were in a happy relationship too?"

I knew this, and at times was insanely jealous of what Bobbie and Peter had. Other times, I was really glad not to be accountable to anyone, and glad to have the freedom to eat Ben & Jerry's with popcorn on my sofa in old sweats while watching Netflix for eight hours straight. I tried to picture Tripp on the other end of the sofa. He filled out a pair of gray sweatpants nicely. Oops, we're relaxing, so no need for a shirt. Chocolate ice cream dripping down an amazing chest I'd partially glimpsed on the basketball court...

I hugged her back. "Do I have tell you you're the best friend in the whole world?"

She eyed me over the rims of her glasses. "I harp because I care."

"I know. I'm trying to embrace my fate but guard my heart at the same time. There's no harm in proceeding this way, no matter how many books it takes."

Bobbie made a face. "Just please, no more that are this boring."

"I promise. Maybe we can upgrade to something a little racier next time."

****

I'm not saying reading-in without the benefit of foreknowledge made me nervous, but I wasn't terribly disappointed that I didn't get a chance all week to sit and read. I kept busy at the shop during the days and my evenings were more hectic than usual. My parents passed through town and stayed a night, and the Upper Orrington business district association held their quarterly meeting, where I got to visit with Gregorio. He hoped to show the shop and apartment to his mom's friend sometime on Friday.

On the evenings I stayed home, I could hear Gregorio next door working late hours. I didn't want to accidently drag him into my story again. Not that the construction next door kept me awake all week, but by Friday, I was glad to be in bed by eight, knowing that showing a rental to a possible tenant would be a quiet activity.

I was asleep before my head hit the pillow.

****

Pom Squad Mystery #17???

Beth pulled her FHA sweater more tightly around her body as the wind blew stray leaves across the sidewalk. *I'm certainly not dressed for rain*, she thought, as she appraised the clouds overhead. The park wasn't much farther. If Steve was on time to meet her, they'd be able to make it to the library before any nasty weather broke out.

Their goal for today was to find out information about the time capsule itself. Other than a rival school prank, she could only think of one other motive for the theft. There was something inside that capsule that someone didn't want revealed. But to figure it out, she needed to know what it contained.

That didn't mean she'd ignore the rival theory, but a good sleuth knew to follow up on all potential leads. Since Sandy was busy today, Steve had agreed to help her with the research.

Another thing that puzzled Beth was the fact that she was here at all. She had no recollection of picking up *Pom Squad Mystery #17* before going to bed, in fact, she had been doing her utmost to avoid it altogether, to be honest.

Beth shrugged. So now the legacy was invading her dreams. Oh well, at least this way when she made a fool of herself, Tripp wouldn't actually be there to witness it. It would be interesting to see how it played out. Would Tripp be Steve, or himself? Maybe this was the legacy's way of giving her a heads-up of what was to come.

Penny heard the steady beat of a basketball on concrete as she turned the last corner. Steve wasn't dressed to play, but he was always prepared to shoot a few hoops when he had extra time on his hands. When he saw her, he stopped; holding the ball, he waited for her to approach.

"I didn't know if you'd be here."

I couldn't decipher the odd expression on his face. I hoped dream-Penny would have an easier time talking to dream-Tripp, or dream-Steve, or whoever we were.

"Well, sure. We're going to the library, right?"

He gave me another weird look. "Penny?"

"Tripp! Oh good, I didn't know who we'd be in my dream. I thought I was Beth for a few minutes. This is totally crazy, right? I've never dreamed about you or book-world before. Of course you aren't my Tripp anyway, you're dream-Tripp, thank goodness, otherwise all this babbling would be really embarrassing."

Tripp ran his hand through his hair, squeezing the back of his neck in an agitated manner, which I'd come to recognize as a stressed-Tripp move. "Penny. This isn't a dream."

"Of course it is. I didn't read us in, I fell right to sleep. You're dream-Tripp, so you can't really know." I grabbed the basketball from where his other arm was bracing it against his hip. "Watch, I'm pretty sure dream-me can sink this shot." I heaved the very un-dream-like basketball toward the opposite end of the court. It sailed through the air, falling several feet, okay, several yards, short of the hoop. "Huh," I said. "Oh well, that probably wasn't a fair test of my R.E.M. anyway."

Tripp put his hand on my arm. "Penny, stop for a minute. I did this."

"What?" I turned to face him.

"I did this. I read us in."

"What?" I said again dumbly.

"I ordered the books from eBay. I couldn't remember which one exactly, so I started reading number thirteen, I read about the first couple chapters of books thirteen through sixteen till I got to this one. Lucky number seventeen."

"Why?"

"To try to wrap my brain around the whole situation a little and to prepare a little for our dates." He blushed lightly.

"You did this? You read us in?" My mind spun through the ramifications. Bobbie would flip out over this addition to her notebook. "Wait. Were you trying to cheat?" I frowned. "Bad form!"

He held up his hands in defense. "What? No!"

"Yes, you totally were. You were going to read ahead and solve the mystery and come off looking like the hero in my book." Okay, so maybe in my excitement I departed from reality just a smidge.

Tripp placed both hands on my shoulders and forced me to meet his gaze. "No. I was only trying to understand what is happening to us better. You know it's not really real, and the ridiculous mystery will get solved with or without us doing anything. Take a breath."

I did. "I'm sorry, this is very disconcerting." It was my turn to give him an apologetic look. "I guess this is how it must be for you every time I drag you in. It's weird not having any time to prepare."

He laughed. "Believe me, I wasn't exactly prepared this time either. Did you know I could, you know…?" Tripp gestured around us.

"No, I don't think it's ever come up before. What are the chances of the guy just happening to pick up the same book one of my grandmothers was reading?" I smiled at him. "About the same as you randomly picking up this book."

"For one, they were pretty hard to find. I paid more for the set than anyone in their right mind would, not to mention expedited shipping."

I giggled. Sue me.

"Yes, hilarious. The worst part was reading through the first chapters of five of them without vomiting. I get down on my knees...well, let's just say I'm eternally grateful not to be a pre-teen girl who would actually be riveted by this drivel."

"Harsh. I enjoyed these when I was younger. I'm sure one day my daughter will too. They're not trashy." I blushed as I remembered my one-day daughter might also be his.

He smiled at me and pulled me in for a hug and kissed the top of my head. "Just don't make me read it for a bedtime story. I want that in our prenup."

His joke about our shared fate sent my stomach butterflies aloft. Neither of us was ready to embrace it, but we weren't rejecting it out of hand.

"So where do we go from here?" I asked into his warm chest.

He released me but held onto my hand, gently leading me up the sidewalk. "The library."

****

"So where are you right now?" I asked as we left the park and headed toward town. I admired the perfectly manicured town. Trash didn't litter the streets and every building sported a cheery welcome sign.

"What do you mean? I'm here, with you."

"No, I mean your real-life body."

A lightbulb came on. "I'm at work, in my office."

"Are there any other people around?"

"No, I closed alone tonight. Why?"

"I have to be careful when I read-in. Anybody close-by ends up going with me. Bobbie and Peter come with me on purpose, but one other time there was...an incident."

49

"I'm not always alone when you drag me in. Sometimes I'm in the middle of a conversation with a customer. That's awkward, at least for me. I'd like to think I cover well. What kind of incident?"

"You can imagine, I don't go around sharing this part of my life, for obvious reasons."

Tripp nodded in agreement.

"Well, one time, my neighbor accidently came with us, so I ended up having to explain the whole thing."

"I don't remember that. She must be a fairly open-minded person."

"You hadn't self-realized yet, and we managed to get him off-scene before you showed up."

"Him. So, a guy neighbor. You were lucky then. Women tend to be more open-minded about hokey stuff like this."

"What's that supposed to mean? You've been fairly open-minded about it."

"I'm not like other guys." He grinned and bumped my shoulder.

We arrived at the same malt shop from the other evening after the game. The overhead bell tinkled as what could only be described as a greaser stumbled out on to the sidewalk in front of us. A girl followed him. Not exactly a girl. She was obviously with him; the painted-on capri pants and leather jacket placed them as a couple. But the rest? Oh my. Her hair was completely pewter-gray with several pure white streaks. It was swept up into a ponytail, high on the back of her head, with strategically escaped ringlets curling at her temples. The bright red scarf tied around her neck perfectly matched the lipstick that was slowly bleeding into the wrinkles around her lips. She batted her mascara-encrusted eyelashes at me before assuming an expression of bored contempt. She wasn't an unattractive woman by any means but dressing like someone forty years younger was not a look I'd recommend for anyone.

Finally, I turned my attention to the greaser.

"Penelope? What have you done now?"

I had to admit, Gregorio wore "bad boy" exceptionally well. "Hey there, neighbor," I gave him a little wave.

"*This* is the neighbor?" Tripp tightened his grip on my hand.

"This is *the* guy?" Gregorio smirked and ran his hand casually through his hair, which really looked much the same as it normally did.

Tripp scowled at him.

"Tripp, meet my neighbor, Gregorio. Gregorio, this is Tripp, *the* guy."

They grudgingly shook hands, barely refraining from squeezing the life out of each other.

"It is a pleasure to meet you. Penelope's mentioned you a time or two."

"Whereas I, just two minutes ago learned of your existence," Tripp responded with a smug smile.

Time to change the subject. "Who's your friend, Gregorio? I can't believe she belongs here."

"Ah, yes. Remember I told you I'd be showing the apartment today? This is Cora, my godmother."

"I promise, this was a total accident. I'm actually in bed, asleep. Tripp read me in this time."

Gregorio's eyebrows flew up as he shot a glance at Tripp. "Really? Bobbie will be most interested in this development."

At this point, Cora inserted herself into the conversation. "You Warriors won't even know what hit you." She blew a small bubble with her gum and popped it sharply. "The Cavaliers will wipe the court with you, plus another little surprise," she chuckled snidely to herself.

"That was NOT my Aunt Cora," Gregorio said.

"Um, okay. I gather that was script. You probably need to get her out of here, otherwise she's going to self-realize and you'll have a lot of explaining to do," I told him.

"You tell ''em, Billy!" Cora encouraged Gregorio, who hadn't told anybody anything. Then she said, "I'm coming, baby," and proceeded to stroll over to a classic-looking black convertible and get in. She slammed the heavy door and, after settling in her seat, pulled out a file and began to shape her fingernails.

"I guess that's your cue to leave." Tripp draped his arm over my shoulders.

Gregorio scowled at him, which complemented his overall look, then turned back to me. "Penelope, I can't wait to hear all about the escapade." He paused and pinned Trip with a pointed glare. "When I see you." A feral grin spread over his face. "Tomorrow." He leaned over and brushed a kiss across my cheek before striding to Billy's car.

"There was no need to be rude." I shrugged Tripp's arm off my shoulder after Gregorio pulled away. Why didn't he just pee on me and be done with it?

"That's a mid-1950s Buick Skylark," he said almost to himself. "As if I didn't need another reason to hate the guy." He ignored my comment. "What's your deal with him? He was way too familiar to be 'just a friend.'"

I tried to sound casual. "We dated. Just a couple of times."

"Who ended it?"

"Not that it's any of your business, but I did. Having a real relationship was not exactly compatible with whatever we have going on here. I thought about how I'd feel if you were dating someone." I shrugged. "I didn't like the feeling, so I told Gregorio we should just be friends."

Tripp's body relaxed. "He doesn't look much like a shopkeeper. I was surprised, that's all."

"Technically, he's not. His late uncle ran the shop. Gregorio's in construction and he's been remodeling the place. The older woman, Cora, is thinking about renting. He showed her the apartment this evening. I guess they weren't finished.

Tripp was silent for a moment. "You're right. I don't like the feeling either." He reclaimed the hand. "Let's get to the library."

We reached the library in another short block, then climbed fifteen marble steps to a pair of grand oak doors. "Not very handicap compliant, is it," I joked.

"Why would it matter? Neither of our characters is disabled." Tripp's tone was flat. I wondered if he was still grumpy about my past relationship with Gregorio.

"It was just an observation. It's not integral to the plot. Besides, I don't think the laws were as strict in the era this story takes place, and certainly not in whatever year this monstrosity was fictionally built."

"Disabled people rarely showed up in books unless the book was about being disabled."

"I'm not going to disagree with you, and I don't know that now is the time to have a philosophical discussion about it," I said carefully, not understanding Tripp's weird mood. He was acting like a tired child. I wondered idly, since I was still asleep in my bed, if I'd wake up when I returned this time. Would I remember my time here, or forget it like a dream? More notes for Bobbie's book.

Tripp grunted, but seemed to throw off his bad mood like a coat. He yanked open the heavy door and ushered me inside.

The smell of old books hit me as soon as I crossed the threshold. It reminded me of my shop, but with fewer dusty overtones. The lobby was dark, and oppressively oak. In fact, all walls, molding, and doorways were made out of the dark-stained wood. The ceiling, high above us, was a light plaster of some sort. From it hung an ornate brass chandelier that cast everything in a slightly yellowish hue. The dark walls absorbed most of the overhead light, requiring several floor lamps to be placed throughout next to equally dark leather club chairs.

To my right, a wide hallway led to a lighter space, and I could see short bookshelves and tiny chairs. To my left was an identical hallway that led to a large room full of work tables. As my eyes adjusted, I realized the lobby walls were not plain wood, but column upon column of tiny drawers. A real, honest-to-goodness card catalog. Dewey decimal, don't fail me now.

Our feet echoed as we crossed the marble tile to the built-in circulation counter. Several women, stereotypically all wearing glasses and buns, were behind the oak counter sorting books or stamping cards. Occasionally, one would disappear into the tall shelves behind the desk, where I assumed special volumes were housed. The women moved on silent feet. After Tripp and I stopped, the only sounds were the slaps and slides of books being stacked and the thump of the rubber stamp.

"Excuse me," my voice thundered. Not really, but it sounded really, really loud.

"May I help you?" the bespectacled woman in the gray cardigan asked.

"Yes, please. May we look at your microfiche?"

She looked at me over the top of her rims. "What year and month?"

"Um…" I did rapid subtraction in my head. "1933, September through November."

"The local Chronicle or the Times?" The librarian character lacked depth. She neither smiled nor judged us. She was perfunctory.

"Definitely the Chronicle."

"One moment please." She jotted my request down on a scrap of paper and retreated to the back. She returned an impossibly short time later with three small yellow envelopes. "The reader is through there." She gestured toward the room with the tables. "Make sure your hands are clean. Return them to me when you've finished."

"Yes, ma'am," I answered automatically. We left the desk, but Tripp turned back.

"May I borrow a sheet of paper and a pencil?" He turned on the charm. I should have told him to save his breath. She wasn't scripted to have depth.

Pu-lease. The woman actually blushed as she handed over the requested items. Tripp charmed personality out of a scene extra. "Thank you, Miss Hatcher," Tripp said, glancing at her name tag. "I'll be sure to return the pencil when we bring back the films."

He caught back up to me. "We might need to write down what we find out," he explained.

"I should have my notebook in my purse. You can't take it back with you, you know."

"I know, but writing stuff down helps me remember it. I was serious about actually trying to solve this thing."

I smiled at him, relieved he'd pulled out of his funk. "Great! Now, do you know how to work this thing?" We'd reached the only high-tech piece of equipment in the room. And by high-tech, I really meant the only thing not made out of wood or marble. It still qualified as a dinosaur.

"I think it's pretty straight-forward. Slide the film in here and flip the switch there on the side."

I did so and the screen lit up. I placed the first film on the tray and slid it into the machine. A bunch of tiny squares appeared. Tripp adjusted the knobs on the side and the squares became big and blurry. After a few more turns, I could make out the headlines. "Hold it there. Let me see if the headlines tell us anything before I try to comb through individual pages."

"If you're all set here, I'm going to go ask where they keep old yearbooks." He jabbed his thumb back at the circulation desk.

"Good idea. Just go easy on the charm. You don't want to give anyone heart palpitations."

Tripp gave me a mock salute before turning on his heel and heading back to the lobby.

I refocused on my task. There had to be a clue here, because this is where Beth had been heading. I hoped it would be obvious that I was on the right track. How embarrassing would it be for a couple of twenty-somethings to not be able to solve a pre-teen simple mystery? Not finding anything in the September edition, I replaced the film with the October slide. I scanned the headlines. Pay dirt. *Class of 1933 Prepares Time Capsule*. I enlarged the page so I could read the article.

Chapter 8

Shoot for Two

Pom Squad Mystery #17

The yearbooks had been easy to obtain, I didn't even need to turn on the charm. As I headed back to show Penny my prize, I noticed a man, noticing me. He was tall and lanky, with thinning hair trimmed close to his head. He held a broom and the brown shirt and pants barely clinging to his frame identified him as a janitor. I stopped and stared back at him. I didn't know this guy's problem, but if he was trying to be unobtrusive, he failed. I didn't get a creepy old guy vibe from him, but then he smiled at me like he knew me.

"A hello to you as well, Steven," the man said.

Okay, then. Story line. I thought to myself. I looked at his collared work shirt, the name tag just said "Lewiston." He started talking again even though I'd failed to respond. As before, it didn't appear to matter whether I actively participated or not. The story would go on as long as I stood there.

"I only work at the school during the week. Saturdays I work at the library. Great benefits, all the free books I want." He laughed at his own joke.

Lewiston. This must be the famous Mr. Louie, one of our prime suspects.

"Yes, yes. That was bad business at the school this week. Not just the missing time capsule, but the leaking sprinkler system, too. It ran most of the night before I discovered the leak yesterday morning."

That sounded like a clue. I'd have to remember to tell Penny.

"Not to worry, son. You win a few more games like the one last night and the finals will be in the bag," Mr. Louie reassured me, even though I had no recollection of playing in a game last night.

"All right, then. You take care, now. I'll see you at school Monday," he said, then turned away from me and resumed sweeping.

I stared after him for a moment, then shook my head at the absurdity of my situation.

I found Penny hunkered down over an antique microfiche reader. She scribbled notes on a scrap of paper provided for that purpose. I watched her in this unguarded moment. I couldn't believe she'd one day be my wife. That part of my life had not even been on my radar yet. True, I was unbelievably attracted to her, found her funny and easy to talk to, but I'd never gone into a relationship already knowing the endgame. We were trying to get to know each other, but the word *wife* loomed large in my mind. She'd been completely open with me about everything I asked. It wasn't fair of me not to do likewise. I just needed more time.

I came up behind her and rested a hand on her waist. She startled, then leaned back into me.

"How's it going?" I asked.

She turned and I backed off, giving her space. "Not bad. They assembled the capsule during a big ceremony. The article mentioned that the graduating class contributed items but didn't say specifically what. It did say that each senior student had to write a 'what I'll be doing in 25 years' paragraph to include. It also said a complete list of items was given to the mayor to keep for posterity. Did you get the yearbooks?"

I held them up. "1932 and '33."

"I think we'll only need '33. The capsule was assembled in October of 1933. The graduating class of '33 returned during homecoming to add their items. Oh, and I don't know if I mentioned it or not, but your dad, well, Steve's dad, is the mayor. So that will be our access to get the list of capsule items."

I raised an eyebrow. "Convenient."

"I know, right?" She grinned.

"I ran into Mr. Louie a minute ago."

Penny looked around me toward the lobby. "Here? That's weird."

"Not so much. It appears they don't pay school employees any more in the fictional 1950s than they do in real life. He's the janitor here on Saturdays."

"Did he say anything important? He must have, otherwise he wouldn't be in this scene."

"Maybe. He mentioned the sprinkler leak and that it probably ran all night, so anyone entering the building would have mud on their shoes. He seemed way more concerned about that than the time capsule. I don't think he's our guy; too nice."

"You're probably right," she agreed. "Too many signs point to him. We're not far enough into the story for the solution to be that simple. Let's look at the yearbook."

I led her to one of the study tables and pulled out a chair for her. She gave me a smirk that I couldn't decipher. There was a lot I didn't know about her. Was she laughing at my chivalry or was she some ultra-feminist who'd rebuff my effort under normal circumstances? Either way, she took the seat and allowed me to scoot her in.

"Thank you," she murmured, already opening the yearbook.

I took a seat beside her and leaned in to see the pages.

"No way!" She flattened the pages out and squinted to read the caption on the photo that caught her attention. "'Frederick Dunn and Eloise Frank crowned prom king and queen 1933, One Enchanted Evening.'"

"Isn't that…"

"Yes! The principal and librarian were part of the class of 1933, and it looks like they were a couple!" Penny rubbed her hands together with excitement. "This has to be what we were meant to find."

It tickled me to see her so excited about her discovery; she was really getting into this. "Let's see if they were involved in any other activities."

We quickly scanned through the pages, finding their senior cap and gown photos, as well as their names mentioned in a couple of candids. They were obviously quite the power couple that year.

"Frank was on the pom squad," Penny pointed out.

"Looks like Dunn was the varsity basketball team captain." I scanned through the gray-tone action shots, my mind supplying the school colors as I went. Only a few were Dunn in his white uniform with red trim. The rest of the photos were mostly of another guy wearing a red uniform with white trim. Penny spoke before I could read the captions.

"Listen to this, 'JV captain Louis Lewiston leads his team to victory against the Bulldogs,' Mr. Louie went to school here too!"

I read the rest of the page. "It looks like he was a sophomore, so he wouldn't have anything to do with the time capsule. No motive."

"Maybe he was secretly in love with Eloise; maybe he still is!"

"That's still not a motive. By stealing the capsule, he would have just made her job more difficult. That's not a very good seduction strategy."

Penny batted her eyelashes and spoke in a sing-song voice. "Maybe he did it so he can miraculously find it later and play the hero."

"Then he doesn't deserve her. A good guy wouldn't use deception to make his girl sad, just so he could save the day later. That doesn't happen in real life."

Penny's eyes filled with mirth. "Tripp, you're killing me. I can't decide if I should swoon over your romantic rationalization or bust a gut laughing when I remind you that this isn't real life." She gasped, then proceeded to laugh her ass off at my expense. Nice.

"I'm sorry," she said when she'd caught her breath. "That really was romantic, though. From what you've told me about your encounter with Mr. Louie, he doesn't strike me as a conniving guy."

"You've got one team captain that ended up a principal and another that's the underpaid janitor. They obviously made different life choices. Louie seems pretty simple; it could be he was just best suited to be a janitor. It's honest work."

"But not work that pays well. Maybe there's some animosity between him and Dunn. Maybe Eloise doesn't factor in at all, maybe he resents Dunn for having a better position," Penny suggested, again with the evil plot theories.

"I'm not sure where else this scene needs to go; do we need to make a plan to meet again?" I asked.

"I was afraid to read-in too soon after the last time. I didn't want to come on too strong. If we're dating, shouldn't we wait a few days between seeing each other? I usually need a few days to process after a read-in," Penny said.

"This isn't anything like a normal relationship. I don't want to risk dragging your neighbor in again. Can we exchange cell numbers? I'm not ready to meet in real life, but texting would be okay, I think."

Penny reached for her back pocket then stopped. "Beth doesn't have a cell phone. Maybe I can write it on my hand."

I reached across my desk and grabbed a pen from the pencil cup my niece had made me.

"Crap," I said out loud to my empty office.

Chapter 9

In which I refuse to believe in coincidences

I awoke Saturday morning with the oddest sensation of not having slept, though I didn't even wake up when I was evicted from my latest book walk. My eyes were gritty and my bladder was full; a sure sign I had, indeed, slept through the night.

Despite my fatigue, a tremor of excitement hummed through me. I jumped out of bed and hurried through my bathroom routine, anxious to catch Bobbie when she came to open the shop that morning. I couldn't wait to share the latest development.

"I don't believe it." Bobbie reached for her notebook. She had been surprised when I greeted her at the shop door this morning. I rarely passed up the opportunity to sleep in.

"I was shocked, too. But I promise, it really happened."

"It could have been a dream. Did you fall asleep with the book on your bed?"

"There's no way it was a dream, but I can't very well open the book up to check, can I?" I handed her my copy of *#17* before she could ask for it.

She found my marked spot and quickly skimmed through the pages. "Was there a scene at the diner?"

"Um, about that, since I wasn't in control, I couldn't plan for a time when the shop next door was empty."

Bobbie groaned. "Don't tell me Gregorio was pulled in again."

"Okay. I also won't mention that the woman he was showing the shop to was there as well."

She stopped reading and looked at me in alarm.

"It's all right. She didn't self-realize, and they weren't there for very long."

"What did Tripp and Gregorio think of each other?"

"Let's just say I've had as much male posturing as I can stomach for a while. They didn't come to blows, but Gregorio used his 'good friends' status a little too liberally. I'm not very impressed with either of them." Our time in the library softened my annoyance at Tripp, but Gregorio and I needed to have words.

"So, do you need to go over and debrief him this morning?" Bobbie asked.

An inappropriate image flashed through my mind. "What?!"

"Good grief! That's not what I meant," she said, realizing how I'd interpreted what she said. "Talk to him and make sure everything was okay with his renter upon their return, is what I meant." She rolled her eyes at me.

"No. I mean I will eventually, but I'm still irritated with him. If there's a major problem, he'll probably come by sometime today. You can just send him upstairs to see me."

I quickly filled her in on how Tripp managed to acquire the book and how far we'd gotten in the chapter. The coffee maker finished brewing, so I made myself a to-go cup to take back upstairs with me.

Bobbie replaced the bookmark and handed me the book. "The next chapter is a squad slumber party, but it's just a cover so Beth and Sandy can sneak out with the boys and investigate at school. Do you want Peter and I to come?"

"Yes, please. It's weird talking to the character who's supposed to be you when you're not there. We can call it a double date!"

She consulted the calendar on her phone. "We can probably do Monday night after you close."

"Can we make it after dinner instead? That way Gregorio will be gone for the day and Tripp will be off work." I wanted to spare him the awkwardness of popping in and out of our story while running his business. "I don't know what time he closes up shop, but around eight on a Monday night shouldn't be too busy for him, I don't think."

"That will work. Peter and I will catch an early dinner on the way over. Want us to bring you anything?"

"No thanks." I headed toward the stairs. "Let me know if you need my help today. I'm just going to be working on the soul mate research and will definitely need a break."

"No way. I can handle things just fine. You get busy on finding our boy." She grinned, shutting the door to the stairwell in my procrastinating face.

The sounds of saw and nail gun haunted me throughout the day. I was determined to not see Gregorio today since he had made the point to tell Tripp that I would. In the meantime, the mystery of Gerald Cleary beckoned.

To be thorough, I continued searching through the church records to make sure Gerald didn't pop back up.

I noticed the schoolteacher during most of that time was William O'Cionnaoith. He must have been bachelor number three. I made a note and copied those pages to a new document, which hopefully, I wouldn't have to pursue.

My diligence paid off. Gerald resurfaced in the 1770 documents, married to Evelyn. Why was that name familiar, and why did Gerald disappear for so long? Off sowing his wild oats before settling down, probably. The name Evelyn nagged at me.

The website I'd been using to search the church records had handy links to find baptisms, deaths, and marriages. There tended to be large holes in the data available, but overall, the amount of information available impressed me.

I entered Gerald's name and approximate dates the marriage would have occurred.

"No. Way."

I reached for the box where I'd stashed my own family tree information and dug to the bottom. Finding the paper I wanted, I scooted my chair back from the table and stood. My spidey sense was tingling. I double checked names and dates three times before donning shoes to go share my find with Bobbie.

I paused with my hand on the doorknob. How far would this go? How many more coincidences before a carefully constructed, albeit gypsy magic constructed, plan emerged? If I shared this with Bobbie now, we'd still have more questions than answers. I slid my shoes back off and returned to my laptop. I sent her a quick text.

--Come up and see me after you lock up. Exciting find!!--

Gerald Cleary had married Evelyn Garvey. Daughter of Elizabeth and Danior, younger sister to my ancestor, Patrick Garvey. She was born after Sarah, making her younger than her own niece. I bet the pregnancy surprised her parents. This also explained why Sarah inherited the legacy instead of Evelyn, an accident of birth.

Did this mean the descendants of Joseph the shop owner were distant relatives of mine? Did that exempt them from being soul mate candidates, or were we far enough removed that it didn't matter? If so, how many more generations down from me would this go before they finally hooked up? Maybe the tree already re-merged and one of my past grandfathers was a descendant of Gerald and Evelyn. It was a long shot, but it sure would make for a tidy tree, in a Hatfield & McCoy sort of way.

I looked back at the book holding my tree information. My rush of energy melted away while I contemplated the daunting task ahead of me. After the teaser I sent, I needed more than the one marriage to show Bobbie. I'd better have lunch before digging back in.

As the afternoon wore on, I made another exciting discovery, followed by guesswork and dodgy theories. Gerald and Evelyn were missing from the 1775 church documents, but their names were listed on the same ship manifest as William and Sarah. They sailed to America together, they were friends, or at least relatives, so it made sense. Not really a coincidence, but it was a satisfying discovery.

They were harder to track once arrived in the U.S. Evelyn had nine kids! I crossed my fingers and continued to track the firstborn male. With Evelyn being Elizabeth's daughter, I considered following the firstborn girl line, but decided against it. I could always backtrack if I needed to. It's not like these people were going anywhere.

I hit a dead end in 1832 when the Cleary branch I followed failed to produce any boys. Jacob and Laura Cleary had three daughters. I glanced at the clock and was shocked to discover it was almost closing time. I stretched and got up to put on a pot of coffee for when Bobbie got there. I knew she had plans with Peter for dinner, so I made scrambled eggs and toast for myself while the coffee brewed.

Bobbie arrived, letting herself in through the door that led to the shop stairs, as I was pouring my cup.

"I've barely been able to focus all afternoon. What's your big news?" she asked, taking the mug I offered her.

"All roads lead back to Elizabeth and Danior."

"That's cryptic. Explain." She added creamer and sugar to her cup.

"Well, not entirely accurate, I was going for mysterious. But this road, the shopkeeper, does lead back to them. Joseph Cleary's son married Elizabeth's daughter!"

"That's a really crazy coincidence. Did you find the heir then?" She took a sip then added more creamer.

"No, but get this. The son, Gerald, and his wife came to America with Sarah and her husband." I barely kept that bottled up all afternoon.

Bobbie settled down in my chair to read over my computer notes. She came to my stopping point and tapped the screen where I'd listed the Cleary daughters.

"That's a wrinkle in your theory. What are you going to do?"

"I'm going to set it aside for a while. My back hurts and I'm getting a headache from deciphering faded and stained handwritten documents. I wish they'd hurry up and invent the typewriter."

"Hmm, not until 1874," Bobbie mumbled distractedly, still reading my notes.

I rolled my eyes but kept silent while she read.

"Who's William O'…Coin…ith?" She'd noticed the other file I'd started.

"Yeah, I don't know how to pronounce it either. He's the schoolteacher. I found some info on him while I was looking into the Clearys. I figured I'd better save it now, so I don't have to hunt for it later. But I'm really hoping the Clearys will lead to the guy."

"Unless one of these ancestries leads directly to Tripp, you won't have any way to know which one is the right one."

Crud. I hadn't thought of that.

"You'll have to leave both of the genealogies with your own grandmother letter."

"If that's the case, I'll need to go back and trace down *all* of the kids and every possible scenario," I whined. "It may be foolish, but I'm just going to pin my hopes on this one. The fact that we have common ancestors is really a minor point. After all, don't we all share common ancestors if we go back far enough." I was feeling a bit desperate.

Bobbie finally realized that the amount of research involved, while exciting to her, was completely stressing me out. She got up and gave me a big hug.

"Hey." She rubbed my back. "It's okay. Don't stress. Cleary is probably definitely the guy. You made a ton of progress today." She changed the subject. "Business was brisk. That display you set up really helped thin down our cookbook inventory. We'll have to assess stock and see what we can replace it with for next Saturday. Oh, and Gregorio stopped by looking for you."

"What did he say?" I stepped out of her hug.

"I told him you were super-busy researching today, then we chatted about last night's read-in."

"Did he mention Cora?"

Bobbie laughed. "Yes, fortunately, she didn't notice anything happened. She's still unsure about renting though, said the space had a 'weird vibe.' So maybe she sensed a little residual strangeness from being in the 1950s."

"Is that all he said?" I resaved my research and closed my laptop.

"He tried to pump me for information about Tripp. He may have thought he was being subtle about it, but he didn't do a very good job of hiding his animosity. It was kind of funny, actually."

"They did not get on at all, so the feeling is mutual. Oh well. I had no control over this one. I need to get Tripp's number next time, so we can coordinate and make sure we don't pull anyone in who doesn't belong."

Bobbie washed out her empty mug and set it in the rack to dry. "Sounds good. Get some rest and stop stressing about the research. I know it's a lot, but you know how the saying goes about how you eat an elephant."

"I know, I know. Blindfolded."

Chapter 10

Sleuthing

With the onset of summer, I began opening the shop on Sunday afternoons to take advantage of locals and tourists enjoying afternoon walks. Gregorio found me, toiling over a gardening display table. The doorbell tinkled, but I was so focused on my task, his greeting startled me.

"Don't do that!" I spun around.

"I apologize. I see you are busy. Shall I come back later?" He shoved his hands in his pockets.

"No, it's fine." I arranged the last few books from my pile. "What's up?"

"I wanted to see how your, ah, trip went. Your friend seems like kind of a hothead. I wanted to make sure you were all right. I talked to Bobbie yesterday."

"Yes, she told me. As far as Tripp being a hothead, you didn't exactly give a great first impression either." Gregorio had the grace to look a little embarrassed. "We are friends," I stressed. "Tripp and I are maybe, probably something more. I appreciate your being protective of me, but your behavior brought out the same instinct in him," I explained, patting his arm to soften the scolding. "I have every confidence the legacy would not pair me with someone who would not be good for me."

He wrinkled his brow. "I admire your faith in the mysterious."

"It was hard to come by, and I still question it frequently. But I have an extensive written history telling me everything will work out." My confident smile was as much for me as for him. "Bobbie mentioned Cora is still unsure about renting."

Gregorio sighed and ran an agitated hand through his hair. "Yes, she said she felt a 'weird vibe,' and would like to look again in a few days. It would be easiest for me to have her as a tenant. I don't normally like playing Realtor or landlord, but I feel she would be an easy tenant, and I wouldn't mind doing landlord things for her since she is like my family."

"Well, hopefully that connection to you will make her decide in your favor. I don't think you ever told me what she wants to do with that much space. It seems large for a one-person insurance office."

"Something with candles, yoga, and nutritional counseling."

I laughed. "That's pretty vague."

"It's something she's been doing on the side. It's where her passion lies, according to my mother. She doesn't want to deal with the expense and upkeep of a house and property anymore. Downsizing isn't a necessity for her, monetarily, so I'm not concerned about her being able to pay rent with whatever it is she does."

"That's good, I guess. I'm looking forward to meeting her under normal circumstances."

"I'll bring her by next time then."

"Then I'll try to make sure to provide the normal circumstances." I grinned. "Just be sure to give me a heads-up."

Gregorio and I said our goodbyes after I warned him we were going to try to read-in Monday evening. He agreed to steer clear of the shop, though I sensed he hoped to be invited along. I didn't think Tripp would be excited about me inviting someone I'd dated on our date, so I ignored Gregorio's hints.

I pulled a notepad from behind the counter to help me organize my thoughts. 1. Tripp is athletic and super-fit. 2. Owns a sporting goods store (chain or private?) 3. Comfortable around weapons. I remembered the way he got all professional when we were on the tower with the margrave. Even though the situation appeared dangerous, Tripp kept his cool and approached it with what looked like law enforcement training. 4. Family? I tried to recall if Tripp had mentioned parents or siblings. I'd have to ask tomorrow night, and maybe get some of my other questions answered, too.

****

Pom Squad Mystery #17

Beth finished stuffing her clothing into her bedroll and stood back to admire her work.

"That's very convincing, Beth. It really looks like you're tucked in there," Patty reassured her. They had chosen to have the squad slumber party at Patty's house because her parents were known to go to bed early and be heavy sleepers.

"Thanks, girls," Beth said. "It's important that we look for clues at the high school tonight before anyone has a chance to contaminate the scene of the crime."

"I'm just glad you'll have Steve and Roger there to protect you," said Brenda with a sigh.

Penny rolled her eyes. She wasn't any kind of hard-core feminist, but if the boys weren't already written into the scene, she and Bobbie could have handled their little recon mission on their own.

"They'll be useful in holding our flashlights." Bobbie smirked, clearly on the same page. Brenda just blinked and looked at her funny, cocking her head slightly in a confused manner.

I held my breath. Was Brenda responding to Bobbie's unscripted comment? If so, it was a new development.

"Tee hee," Brenda giggled. "Yeah!"

I looked at Bobbie, who shrugged, as girly conversation resumed around us.

"Let's roll," she said.

Since we would be escaping out the window and down a trellis, we were somewhat appropriately dressed in black pedal pushers. I wore a black short sleeve sweater. Bobbie had on an olive-green blouse with a short, crocheted black cape thrown over her shoulders. I had my doubts about the loafers I was wearing.

"We are going to break our necks trying to climb in these." I slid my foot on the carpet.

She glanced at her own loafer-clad feet. "I think this may be a case of the author writing lines that have little basis in practicality. Honestly, I think we can probably get away with sneaking out the back door."

"Sounds good to me. Ta ta, girls!"

Patty, Brenda, and three other girls watched the window anxiously as we exited through the bedroom door behind them.

"Oh, do be careful!" I heard one of them exclaim as we made our way down the stairs.

We met no opposition as we passed through the house.

"Will we be coming back here?" I asked Bobbie when we reached the back door located in the kitchen.

"If we finish the whole scene we will, but if we get sent back after the important stuff happens, then, no. We should leave the back door unlocked just in case, though."

I tried to decide if it would really matter if we returned to the bedroom at the end of the night or not. Sometimes it was hard to wrap my brain around how the magic worked. When Tripp and I exited the scene at the high school library, it seemed we could remain 'off-script' as long as we wanted with no repercussions if we were working on our relationship.

If Bobbie and I failed to return to the bedroom, we would technically be 'off-script' as well. How long would the magic keep us here before returning us to the real world? I didn't relish the idea of hanging out in the cool evening or trying to climb in the window if we were locked out of the house.

I unlocked the kitchen window and opened it a crack, just in case. Then we carefully shut the kitchen door and crept around to the front of the house to meet the boys. Peter and Tripp were underneath the only lit window, their heads together in deep discussion.

Bobbie put a finger to her lips, then quickly snuck up behind Peter, goosing him in his side. He jumped about three feet in the air. Tripp took a defensive position and, like on the tower in Margrave, reached for a weapon that wasn't there. Interesting.

"Dang it, Bobbie! I could have hurt you." Peter wrapped her in his arms like he hadn't seen her in five days rather than five minutes.

Tripp relaxed, then scanned the yard until his eyes landed on me. I walked toward him, then made the decision to raise my arms, inviting an embrace. If this relationship was going to happen, we needed to be comfortable with each other. He smiled and his eyes warmed before stepping in to accept my offer. He turned his head and kissed my temple.

"Good to see you again, Bobbie," he greeted over my shoulder.

"You as well," she replied.

Tripp released me but caught my hand in his, enfolding it in his warm grasp.

"Peter tells me we're headed to the high school to look for clues." Tripp's thumb traced lazy circles on the inside of my wrist.

"We need to look for footprints in the mushy ground near the entrance or muddy prints nearby." Bobbie planned to keep us on track without giving away any important details. This was supposed to be a date, after all.

Patty's house was conveniently located just a few lots down from the school, so we headed that way, keeping to the shadows. Since Bobbie knew where we were supposed to end up, she and Peter took the lead. We circled around to the rear of the building to a lot signed 'Faculty Parking.'

"So, I guess we need to just look around in the mushy grass underneath all the windows to see if anyone gained access that way?" I questioned. It seemed the most obvious plan, but I didn't want to waste my time if there was something else we were supposed to be doing.

"That's a good place to start," Bobbie agreed, which told me I may find a clue that way, but this excursion had more in store.

The four of us walked down the sidewalk, shining our lights on the grass under each window. The lawn needed mowing, but I didn't notice any obvious indentations under the windows.

"This must be where the sprinkler shut-off is located." Tripp pointed out a metal box-like cover next to an assortment of pipes and gauges sticking up out of the ground. The area around it had seen much more traffic. Deep footprints and indentations that may have been made by knees marred the ground.

"It's where Mr. Louie and Mr. Dunn tried to make repairs," I guessed.

The grass was saturated and the ground split open where the water from the broken pipe burbled up through the soil. The water carried the soil, washing it on to the sidewalk in a slurry. While the ground still retained water, the sidewalk mess had dried over the past couple days. There were prints that only made slight indentations since they were made when the mud was mostly dry. The only other set of visible prints was quite deep, from when the mess was fresh. Most people would avoid stepping in fresh mud, so why did this person walk straight through it?

I motioned for Tripp to come look at the clue. "This mess is from Mr. Louie and Mr. Dunn, and these prints are more recent, from when it started to dry. But look at that print," I said, pointing to the deeper mark. "It was made when the mud was still oozing. Why would someone step in that mess?"

"This shoe would have definitely had enough mud on it to leave what we saw in the library. If it was dark, he might not have noticed the mud, especially if his mind was on burglary." Tripp scrutinized the print. "Or hers. This is small enough to be a woman's shoe."

"But it doesn't match the pumps Ms. Frank was wearing." I recalled the librarian's chic shoes.

"She wouldn't wear pumps to break into a building."

"She wouldn't have to break in. She had a key!" I said triumphantly.

Bobbie and Peter were sitting on the curb talking. I guess it wouldn't have been fair for them to help look for clues since Bobbie already knew where they were. "Bobbie, were we supposed to find anything besides the print?" I called.

She stood up and brushed off her pants. "Nope. Good job!" Then she nudged Peter who also stood up.

"Oh, right," he said. "Ahem. Why is the gym door propped open? It should be closed this time of night."

I laughed at Peter's scripted lines, then looked across the parking lot to the gymnasium rear door, which did indeed appear to be propped open.

I turned to Tripp. "I guess that's where we're headed next."

Chapter 11

Gone Awry

Pom Squad Mystery #17

We all crossed the well-lit parking lot to the gym door. A leather jacket was wrapped through the handles on each side of the door to prevent the latch from connecting. It was the heavy metal type that normally would slam shut automatically, though I did notice that the inside was lacking the press bar required on all fire exits. Another sign of the times I guessed. There were no visible marks of tampering, and the door didn't appear to have been forced open. The mode of entry probably was not as important as the fact that the leather jacket indicated someone inside still planned to use this as their escape route.

Tripp flattened himself to the side of the building and motioned for us to do likewise. I crept up behind him, Peter and Bobbie close behind me. Tripp peeked through the crack at eye level, so I crouched down to see if I could see anything through the bottom part. I could make out bobbing spots of light on the wall near the floor, but also up high. As my eyes adjusted, I could tell that all the action was happening at the opposite end of the court, behind the basketball goal.

"I see three kids. They have a ladder and are trying to remove something from the wall," Tripp reported.

I turned to Bobbie and whispered, "Are we supposed to run in there and stop them?"

"No. Steve can't tell how many there are and doesn't want to put us females in danger."

I rolled my eyes. "What are we supposed to do?"

"Just give it a minute or so, and be ready to stand back."

I resumed my position at the lower door crack just as the overhead gym lights came on. Tripp pulled me back and a yell came from inside— "Hey! What are you kids doing?"—followed by a crash, another yell, and feet pounding toward us across the gym floor. Tripp pushed us all farther back from the door but kept us pinned to the wall. Three teenagers burst through the door next to us, the last pausing to grab his jacket. He glanced up, and I noticed he looked vaguely like Gregorio. He gave me a cocky grin and salute before taking off after his friends.

"Okay, now we go in," Bobbie said, catching the door before it slammed shut.

Tripp hesitated for a split second, then rushed in at the sound of someone calling for help, Peter on his heels. I came in behind, and Bobbie took off one of her shoes to stick in the door. Across the gym, a middle-aged man in a white shirt and necktie was lying on the floor. As Tripp and Peter knelt down to assist him, I surveyed the scene. The ladder was lying on the floor near the man and a big brown fur rug of some sort was hanging askew on the wall behind the goal.

"It looks like the Cavaliers were trying to steal our beloved Warriors buffalo pelt," Bobbie said, helpfully.

As we approached, Peter was talking to the man. Bobbie had obviously prepped him for his role. "Hold still, Coach Turner, we'll call an ambulance." He stood and jogged toward the hall. I could see faint light coming from what was probably the coach's office.

"Those Cavaliers took this prank too far," Coach Turner moaned. "I was working late when I heard noises coming from the gym. Those rascals thought no one was here because they didn't see a car in the lot. I live nearby and often walk to school."

"Just hold still, sir." Tripp kept a hand on the man's shoulder to prevent him from rising. "Help will be here soon. Do you think you can identify any of the kids?"

Coach moaned again. "No, it was too dark, and then one of them landed on me when I startled him off the ladder. I think my leg is broken. Steve, I just don't know what's going to happen to the season if I'm not able to coach."

"Don't worry about that right now. Concentrate on holding still and remaining calm."

Peter rejoined us and almost immediately we could hear sirens in the distance. Bobbie grabbed a chair from the sideline and used it to hold the door open, replacing her shoe. She waved the paramedics to our location.

"So now what?" I asked her.

"We can go anytime now."

"Really? We don't need to stay and give a statement or anything?" Tripp asked as he and Peter joined us.

"Nope. This will be chalked up to a harmless homecoming prank gone awry."

"Huh. Weird," I said. "Well, I guess we can head back to the slumber party, then." We started to head toward the door, following Coach Turner on the gurney. "Wait a minute. What was the point of this scene?" I stopped walking and turned to Tripp who had a contemplative expression on his face. "What do you think?"

He paused, gathering his thoughts before he spoke. "I think, that if the Cavaliers already had the time capsule, they wouldn't need to steal the pelt, too."

Bobbie clapped her hands dramatically. "Good job! Beth and Steve don't make that connection for another two chapters."

****

We walked back to Patty's house hand in hand, several yards behind Bobbie and Peter. I didn't know about double dating in this weird format. I had a hard enough time acting natural when it was just Tripp and me dealing with the other scripted characters. Bobbie and Peter weren't intrusive, per se, but they felt more like an audience to our date rather than participants. Probably because they both knew what was going to happen ahead of time.

"That was fun." Tripp took off his jacket and draped it over my shoulders against the chilly night air.

I snuggled into it, inhaling his scent. "It was, mostly."

"But?"

"But it felt crowded, for a date."

"I have to say, I've never been on a date quite like it before. We have time now. Ask me anything." Tripp held his arms out in an "open book" gesture.

"Okay, where do you live?"

"Uh ah ah. Try something else." He shook a finger at me.

"Tell me about your family."

"My parents are still married and both living. I have two sisters, one married with a little girl, and one just out of college trying to decide what to do with her life. What about you?"

"My parents are also living. They live near—not near me but visited recently. I'm an only child." I could be cagey, too. "Did you always want to be a sporting goods store owner?" I grinned.

"No. Before this I did several years active duty in the Marines." He didn't say anything else and his expression didn't invite more questions along that line. Thankfully, we arrived back at Patty's yard.

"We need to exchange cell numbers so we can coordinate these meetings better," I reminded him. Bobbie came over, and between the two of us, managed to at least temporarily, memorize his number. I planned to look up the area code when I got home to get a clue about where he lived. Bobbie and Peter disappeared around the side of the house, giving us a little privacy for our good-byes.

I turned to him and wrapped my arms around his waist. "Despite what Bobbie said about our progress in solving the mystery, I don't feel like we accomplished anything tonight. We barely had time to talk, and what I did learn about you, doesn't feel like what makes you, you. I'm not making any sense. I'm sorry."

He held me close and spoke into my hair. "You're right. I'm not used to sharing my feelings, and I've kept myself closed-off from people for a long time. But this—" He pulled back and gestured to the space between us. "This is real, isn't it? I don't know how I can feel so connected to you. I almost feel comfortable sharing parts of my life with you that I don't share with anybody. And it scares me so bad that I end up holding back. So, I'm sorry. It's my fault you don't feel like we're making any headway. But I promise you, it is happening, if only in my heart for right now."

He kissed me, so tenderly I almost cried. All of our past kisses had stemmed from relief, attraction, and maybe a touch of lust, but this one was different. He didn't hold himself back from me, and I could feel his pain and his trust in me in that kiss. I wanted to know what hurt him. Our connection was growing, just in a different way than I expected, so I would continue to be patient. I would wait for this man, with his confusing, protected outside, and his tender, hidden inside.

"Don't cry," he whispered, brushing my tear away with his thumb.

"I'm not," I lied, standing on tiptoes to kiss him again. "I'll text you tonight, so you'll have my number too." We couldn't stand out here forever, Bobbie and Peter were waiting.

"Okay, see you soon." He kissed me one last time on the forehead before releasing me. He trailed his hand down my arm and gave my hand a final squeeze as I backed away.

"Oh!" I pulled his jacket off and tossed it to him.

He caught it and tucked it under his arm. His expression unreadable, he watched me go. As I backed around the corner of the house, he tilted his head to stare into the fake night sky.

Chapter 12

Comforts of Home

I released the breath I took before I left for 1950-something. Back in my office, though I'd never truly left, I stretched my legs out and massaged my thighs. No time may have passed, but my body felt like it had been sitting in my chair for a couple hours. I'd pay for it tonight.

I made my way to the front entrance, shutting off any remaining lights as I went. Weekends were busy, but Mondays tended to be slow, so we closed at six. I used the time to catch up on weekly paperwork so I wouldn't have to take it home.

It was tempting to take work home with me, if only to keep my mind occupied, but not a habit I wanted to develop. Burying myself in paperwork during my free time wasn't conducive to letting my family into my life. I needed to stop keeping them at arm's length.

I barely knew Penny, and I'd already hurt her with my reluctance to open up, I can only guess at how my family was hurting. I glanced at my watch and marveled again at the time paradox. It was only seven P.M. but felt closer to ten. Maybe I could score some dinner at Mom and Dad's. Renting their garage apartment did have some advantages.

I maneuvered my truck through the idyllic streets of my parent's' neighborhood, my neighborhood. I noted the difference in seasons between Penny's book world and real life. Late fall there compared to late spring here. Even though tomorrow was a school day, lots of families were out enjoying the weather. Would that be Penny and me someday? The idea still felt like a suit of clothes that didn't quite fit or a new dress shirt that I tried to put on over my head instead of unbuttoning. It was supposed to fit but wasn't anywhere near comfortable yet.

When I pulled into the driveway, my sister, Kaitlyn came out the front door.

She sidled up to my truck. "Hey, brother, what's up?"

"Nada. Is there dinner left?" I swung down from the cab and winced when I landed heavily on my left leg, which had stiffened up again on the ride home. Kaitlyn's brow furrowed briefly in concern, but she knew better than to say anything.

"There's probably a serving or two left if you hurry. Dad knows there's no dessert tonight, so he may well finish off the dish. It's that thing Mom makes with potatoes and hamburger."

"I'd better get in and stake my claim. Where are you headed?" I slammed the door.

"Blind date." She sighed.

"You're going alone?"

"Tripp, I'm a big girl, and one father is plenty. I'm meeting some friends. My date is the cousin of one of them, in town for a few days. Nothing to worry about." Kaitlyn walked around my truck to her little blue bug.

"Not trying to be another father. It's a brother's job to sort out the riffraff and hand out beatings." I locked the truck and set the alarm. "Save a date night for me this week. We can catch a movie." It was time to start making an effort with my family.

Kaitlyn's eyes widened. "Sure. Thursday work for you?"

"That'd be great. Have fun tonight, be safe."

She opened her door and hesitated. "Everything okay?"

Time to step out in faith. "I've got some stuff going on, but nothing bad. Maybe I'll be ready to talk about it by Thursday."

She relaxed. "Okay, I can't wait. Love you, Tripoli."

"You too, Kait-bait." Our pest-names never failed to raise smiles. I watched her drive away and headed to my parent's' front door just as streetlights began to flicker on.

****

"Mom, that was way better than the leftovers in my fridge upstairs." I leaned back in my chair and patted my belly.

"Hmm. Aren't the leftovers in your fridge also from meals I made? I'm just glad you and your dad didn't come to blows over it. Lucky I found a sleeve of cookies in the cabinet."

"You know it's too late to try to change me, Diane!" my father called good-naturedly from the living room, where he was munching his cookies and watching television.

"It's just a matter of time before that sweet tooth catches up to you, old man," my mother returned.

At fifty-five, my dad was still in great shape, but Mom was right, it would catch up with him. My mom still looked good, too, though she probably wouldn't agree. She wasn't slender but was at least on the right side of heavy. When I looked at her, I just saw my mom, and the comforting presence I had always depended on in the past. I could tell she was frustrated at not being able to kiss my adult boo boos, and that she didn't even know the extent of them.

"Thanks for dinner, Mom. I'm going to head upstairs and try to get a workout in before bed."

"Okay, sweetie, anytime." She began clearing the table, and I carried my own plate and utensils to the sink. My pocket chimed and I pulled my cell phone out.

—*This is Penny from the book. LOL*—

I grinned at her reference to the J-Lo song.

—*Who?*—

—*OMG! I'm sorry, wrong number.*—

—*JK, Pen. It's me, Tripp.*—

—*That was mean.*—

—*I'm sorry, couldn't resist.*—

—*Forgiven, this time. Making it an early night. Heading to bed. Goodnight.*—

—*Sweet dreams, book girl.*—

"I haven't seen that expression in ages, honey. I don't know who you're texting, but I already love her." Mom had watched my exchange with Penny from across the kitchen.

"Just Scott from work."

"Don't fib to me. That's all right, you'll share with me when you're ready." She wiped at her eyes, then gave me a hug and kiss on the cheek before seeing me out the door. "Good night, Tripp, love you."

"You too, Ma."

Chapter 13

Won't You Be My Neighbor

Tuesday, I woke with a new determination to track down Joseph Cleary's descendants. I hoped it would keep my mind occupied even though I knew I just invited frustration. I decided to pretend I was Bobbie and approached the research with excitement. It worked for about twenty-seven minutes.

The book shop was surprisingly busy for a Tuesday morning. I set up my workspace at the checkout counter and had to frequently stop to ring up sales or answer questions. I didn't really mind the interruptions. For one, it meant sales, and for two, it helped me avoid my laptop with its fuzzy birth records and faded newspaper articles.

By lunch, I hadn't gotten much further than uncovering married names for Jacob Cleary's three daughters, Anne, Joanna, and Mary. When I raced upstairs to grab leftovers from my fridge, I also dragged my own family history research box back down to the shop with me. Too many names and places were sounding familiar. In fact, some of the documents I looked at this morning, I would swear I'd examined before.

Business slowed down in the afternoon, which helped, because I felt like I was on to something. I needed to focus.

Anne Cleary, the oldest daughter, married Sean O'Shea. They had two daughters, but neither survived to adulthood. I could find no other birth records. They may have simply moved to a different town, but I didn't want to follow that rabbit trail just yet.

Joanna Cleary, daughter number two, married John Grant of Smithton. That name bothered me. I consulted my ancestor folders. Margaret and Edward Franklin also lived in Smithton. A shiver ran up my spine. Margaret was my fourth great-grandmother.

Even though Smithton was a tiny town, they were proud. They had their own little historical society set up in the original town hall. Through the items they posted online, I discovered Joanna and Margaret were part of the same ladies' auxiliary as well as Jane Franklin, who I determined to be Margaret's daughter-in-law. Jane was Hazel's mother. Hazel was my own grandmother's grandmother. This was too much of a coincidence to not be the right path. I didn't even need to look at the third Cleary daughter. I was sure this was it and it would lead me right to present day. I silently thanked the gods of the internet for making this so easy for me.

I sent an email to the Smithton Historical Society requesting more information on the Franklin and Grant families. I also requested information on how to make a donation to their organization to sweeten the pot. If they could provide me at least another one or two generations worth of names and dates, I would totally send them a check.

I decided to quit for the day, pumped up on the hope that the historical society would save me a couple days' worth of work. As I packed up my materials, Gregorio came into the shop, followed by an older woman, who had to be Cora. She looked kind, and very normal, in clothes that were both age and era appropriate. Her gray hair was cropped in a short pixie cut and her minimal make-up was far more flattering than that worn by her greaser alter-ego.

"Good afternoon, Penelope. I hope we are not bothering you." Gregorio glanced around at the few customers perusing the shelves. "I wanted to introduce you to Cora Richmond. She's going to rent the space next door as soon as it's finished."

Cora smiled at me and extended her hand. "I'm so glad to meet you, Penelope. I promise, I'm a quiet neighbor."

I returned her smile as I took her hand. "My pleasure. I'm sure we'll get on just fine. Please, call me Penny. Gregorio is the only one who insists on the formality of Penelope." I winked at him. As Cora released my hand, Gregorio snatched it up, bringing it to his lips and grazing my knuckles.

"Ah, but a Penny is only a bit of copper, and our Penelope is worth far more than that," he said with a devilish grin.

He let go of my hand before I could pull it free, but I gave him a warning look. I didn't need his godmother thinking there was something between us. The better I got to know Gregorio, the easier I found it to friend-zone him. Or maybe I just found him easier to resist as I grew closer to Tripp. Either way, his flirting and alpha-male tendencies toward me needed to stop. I focused my attention back on Cora who had watched our exchange curiously.

"So, Gregorio tells me you do something with nutrition."

"Yes, in a nutshell." She laughed. "I offer whole-body health counseling for women. I design menus and exercise plans based on individual consultations; I'm also trained to facilitate several different relaxation techniques. Moving my business out of my home, I'm hoping to add yoga classes and lease shelf space to a friend who makes organic aromatherapy products. I'm looking forward to the opportunity to do it full time and give up the insurance gig."

I cocked my head. "Aren't you going to be living upstairs? You'll still be working out of your home."

"I guess I will. But it will be easier to delineate the space if I'm not doing consults at my kitchen table."

"Will your business be by appointment only? We do get a fair amount of foot traffic, especially when the weather is nice."

"To start with, yes. But besides the aromatherapy products, I'm going to look for other vendors that make specialized diet and exercise products I might include. I'm excited about the possibilities. The space is big enough for a store front, small studio, and my office. I could also rent the studio out to a massage therapist a couple days a week."

"If you do, I'll be first in line." I could see why Gregorio wanted her as a tenant.

She patted my arm. "Aren't you sweet. I feel so much more comfortable about the move having met you. Your shop is so cozy. I love the positive energy." She turned to Gregorio. "I'm going to take a peek at the shelves. You don't need to wait on me if you've got places to be. Thank you for introducing me to Penny." Cora stood on her tip toes and grabbed Gregorio's face so she could plant a big smooch on is cheek. "Tell your mom I said hello." Then she disappeared into the bookshelves.

"I really like her," I whispered to Gregorio.

"She's the best," he agreed. "How have you been? How's Skip?"

"*Tripp* is good. I've been working on the ancestry stuff today. I think I've had a breakthrough, so it's been a good day."

"I'm glad. So, is all your research going to lead to Trey?"

"In a perfect world, *Tripp* would turn out to be the guy who is the descendant of my distant grandmother's true love, and the legacy would be fulfilled, and my one-day granddaughter won't have to deal with this craziness, and she could date and marry whoever she wanted." I sucked in a breath before continuing. "But most likely it won't lead to Tripp. It'll be good information to pass down, though. If this breakthrough pans out, it could be the guy is very close. There are a lot of parallels emerging between the two families. If I can figure out who they are, I could maybe befriend the woman who ends up being the grandmother of 'the guy.' That sounds a little stalkerish though, doesn't it?"

He smiled. "It's a little creepy, yeah. I'd be willing to vouch for your good intentions in any case."

We stood there awkwardly for a moment before he continued. "I've got to go. I just wanted you to meet Cora, for real this time, and let you know the space was leased." He shoved his hands in his pockets.

"I'm glad she decided to go ahead with it. She seems nice. Thank you for bringing her by."

Gregorio nodded, then backed his way out the door, keeping his speculative gaze on me. Maybe once I figured out my love life, I could help Gregorio get his sorted. He may be a believer in my family legacy, but he seemed to have strong reservations about Tripp being my true love. And if I opened the door even a little bit to the possibility of a relationship, he would bust on through it like the Kool-Aid man.

Chapter 14

Sibling Reveal-ry

"Is that what you're wearing?" Kaitlyn asked as I descended the stairs from my garage apartment.

I looked down at my clean jeans and NRA t-shirt. "What's wrong with it?"

She shrugged. "Nothing, I guess. Good thing you aren't actually my date."

She was dressed in a short, blue halter-dress thing, with a jean jacket in deference to the evening chill. She'd probably still be cold and I'd have to lend her the heavier jacket I keep in the truck when we got to the theater.

"You don't look any different than normal," I made the mistake of saying.

"These wedges are new." She stuck out her foot. "Just because we'll be out together, doesn't mean we won't be noticed. In fact, I'll be in the perfect position to see if anyone is checking you out. Then I can make loud family-related statements so the interested party will know we're siblings and you're available."

"Maybe I should just get a shirt made that says, 'I'm her brother.'"

"Sure, and I'll wear one that says, 'I'm with stupid.' Let's go, I'm starved. Where are you taking me?"

"I was thinking McHenry's." I opened the passenger door and lifted her into my truck. Between the skirt and shoes there was no way she was getting in unaided.

"Ew. No." She pulled the belt over her chest and snapped it in place.

"Why not?" I climbed in and fastened my seat belt while Kaitlyn fiddled with the radio.

"I went out once with a guy who works there. I don't want him to get the wrong idea."

"Okay. Where do you want to go?"

She gave me a side eye. "Your outfit limits us to some extent. Luckily, I'm kind of in the mood for pizza."

"So, Joe's?" I started the engine and the radio blared. I quickly shut it off, and Kaitlyn scowled at me.

"No. Let's do DaVinci's. It's got a better vibe."

"Whatever you say, Princess." I backed out of the driveway. Kait was a fun pain in the ass. I wondered why we didn't do this more often.

****

"Mom says you met someone." Kaitlyn meticulously cut her pizza slice into bite-size pieces. Habits formed after years of wearing braces were hard to give up.

I took a bite of my own slice to avoid the question. I glanced around the room. DaVinci's did indeed have a cool 'vibe.' The inside had been modeled to look like an outside space. It reminded me of places I'd eaten in Italy. I swallowed, then chased it with a gulp of cola.

"What are you going to do now that you have a fancy degree?" I asked, instead of answering her question.

"Business. Not so fancy, but it might come in handy with whatever else I decide to do. Dad wanted me to have something more substantial than just the art stuff. I've got a couple of applications out at places that look interesting. We'll see. I don't mind what I'm doing now, and it pays the bills, so I can wait until the perfect opportunity presents itself." She pointed her fork at me. "See, that's how you answer a direct question like an adult. Who's the girl? The only place you ever go is work, so she must be some kind of gun-toting badass if that's where you met her." She stabbed a bite of pizza and brought it to her lips while continuing to glare at me. She'd make a great mom one day. She almost had our mother's penetrating look perfected.

"It's not a normal situation. I didn't exactly meet her at work. I can't really talk about it." I knew this explanation would not cut it.

"Why can't you talk about it? Is she secret service or something?"

Why couldn't I talk about it? Penny had never given a reason not to, other than the situation being so completely implausible that no one would believe it anyway. It really took some doing to actually have someone committed to an insane asylum these days. Besides, I already had a shrink, and she'd declared me healthy.

"Okay, I *can* tell you. But you won't believe it, and I don't feel like listening to ridicule." I resumed eating.

"All right. Are you really dating her, or is she just someone you like?" Kaitlyn asked.

It looked like I was up for a game of twenty questions. "Yes, to both. In fact, I'll probably marry her." *Oops, should have held that back.*

Kaitlyn reached across the table and smacked me on the shoulder, hard. "What the heck, Tripp?! You can't say things like that about someone you haven't even brought home to meet the 'rents. Who is this woman?"

I sighed. Busted. "Her name is Penny. She has curly brownish hair, I think, and, uh, she likes to read."

"Are you freaking kidding me right now? Where did you meet? What does she do? Where does she live? What is her last name? Basic info, Tripp."

"She owns a used bookstore," I added hopefully. I was beginning to sweat under Kaitlyn's menacing stare. "Okay, I can tell you the story about how we met, but you have to be willing to completely set aside reality. Can you do that? And also, not tell Mom yet."

"I think the fact that I'm willing to entertain the idea of a real woman being in a relationship with you proves I'm willing to set aside reality…or at least rationality." She smirked.

"Remember, you asked for this. Not one word till I finish."

She settled back and continued eating but, gave me her full attention otherwise. I'd have to be ready to perform the Heimlich maneuver when she choked on my story.

"I met Penny during the Renaissance." Kaitlyn opened her mouth, but I held up a finger. "Hold all questions until the end, please."

I told Kaitlyn as much as I could remember about Penny's family legacy, about her grandmothers, and the research she was doing. I told about the *Margrave* book and the book Penny and I were reading now. I told her about Bobbie and Peter, and about how Penny and I were 'dating' but taking it slow. I also explained that because I was slow to give up my own personal information, I hadn't asked or received too much personal information from Penny. By the time I'd finished my tale, the pizza was cold, and we'd missed the beginning of the movie we'd planned to see.

"Now, I'll take your questions."

She leaned in with a feral look in her eyes. "I want in."

"What?!"

"If all you've said is true, and you obviously believe it is, I want to see. You've never been particularly creative, so I don't think you're making it up. You're not one for drugs. You won't even take your pain meds without a fuss. So, I want to see. You said Penny brings her friends in, why can't you? I'm withholding judgment on all of it until I can see, or not see, for myself."

It wasn't the response I was expecting, though knowing Kaitlyn, I probably should have. I'd never considered bringing someone in with me. I didn't have close friends anymore, it made me feel even worse about how I'd discounted my family.

"Let me talk to Penny first and see what's coming up in the book. Not all scenes lend themselves to extras. Her friend, Bobbie, reads ahead so we don't have any major surprises. Though this book is relatively tame."

"Why can't you just read ahead?"

I laughed. "I tried that. Turns out, if it's the same book Penny already started, I can read in as well. Let me tell you, that was a surprise."

"You actually have a copy of the book, right? So, I could read ahead for you," Kaitlyn suggested.

I immediately felt protective of the paperback sitting in my office desk drawer. "I don't know. Probably," I hedged. "We're using the in-book meetings as dates. If you read ahead, you can't tell me what was going to happen."

"Deal. Where's the book? At home? Let's go."

"Wait. No, it's at work, and I'm not stopping by tonight. I'll bring it home with me tomorrow." I still needed to process the idea of Kaitlyn reading it, and also run this whole turn of events by Penny. We hadn't utilized our new cell phone connection other than that first night, but this seemed like a good reason to text her. I was looking forward to it.

Chapter 15

What Happens at City Hall…

I had just settled into bed when my phone dinged. I'd given Tripp his own message alert tone so I would know immediately when he contacted me. That ding had me sitting up in bed and turning on my lamp.

—*You up?*—

—*Sure.*—

—*I told my sister tonight.*—

—*About what exactly?*—

—*Everything.*—

Oh boy. I hoped his sister was open-minded.

—*And how did that go? Did she believe you?*—

—*She wants to see for herself, to meet you. To make sure I'm not crazy.*—

—*Makes sense.*—

—*Do you mind?*—

—*How can I mind when Bobbie and Peter come all the time?*—

—*But it's your thing. You can make the rules to some extent. I didn't want to presume. Kaitlyn's a bit spirited.*—

—*It'll be great. We don't know for sure if you can bring people with you. It doesn't happen when I read you in. You might have to read for her to come. Bobbie says the next scene is just us, we can talk about it then.*—

—When?—
—Friday night?— I suggested.
—Depends. What time?—
—7 okay?—
—What time zone?— Tripp asked.
—Good question. Eastern. Same for you??—
—….—
—???—
—Yeah. 7 Eastern works for me. See you later.—
—Night.— I shut down my phone and turned out the light.

Getting information out of that man was like pulling teeth. I understood his wanting to maintain distance until we were better acquainted, but this really felt like there was something he didn't want me to know. I wouldn't go so far as to say he was hiding something, that sounded too dishonest, and I really didn't get that vibe from Tripp. In fact, he seemed uncomfortable concealing the thing he wasn't telling me.

I flipped my pillow over to the cool side and tried to relax. My brain couldn't help analyzing our text exchange. He wouldn't even admit to a time zone. I had researched his area code and knew it was California area, but that didn't feel right. Not that I know what a person from California is supposed to be like.

He asked if I was up. Eleven o'clock is pretty late to expect a text, so he must have known that. If he were in Cali, it would only be eight o'clock and he wouldn't have thought to ask…unless he knew where I lived. I wracked my brain, trying to remember if I'd shared that information, but I didn't think so. I could assume he was East coast like me or possibly Midwest. I didn't detect an accent. I bet he was East coast like me. That would make sense with my research if he turned out to be 'the guy.' It was awfully pat, though.

I finally drifted off to sleep with a smile on my face with the thought of my date for tomorrow night. Was it love? No, not yet, but it was something.

****

Friday night.

Pom Squad Mystery #17

It was Sunday afternoon when Steve and Beth crept around to the back entrance of city hall. The building was empty, and the young sleuths decided it was the best time to seek out the information they still needed, the contents of the time capsule. Steve pulled the keys from his pocket and inserted the largest one onto the lock.

"Are you sure your father won't miss his keys?" Beth asked nervously.

"He'll be golfing all afternoon. We're perfectly safe," Steve reassured her.

The door opened easily, and the teens quickly entered the building, locking the door behind them.

"This way," Steve said, leading Beth down the corridor.

They reached a heavy wooden door and Steve led them through without hesitating. His father had been the mayor for ten years and city hall was practically a second home to him. It was coming in handy now. Beth would never have had the courage to do this on her own.

They made their way across the marble entrance hall, the rubber soles of their tennis shoes silent in the cavernous space. Steve pulled out his keys again, this time dropping them on the floor. Penny jumped as the noise echoed throughout the room.

"Sorry," Tripp whispered, though his voice also echoed. He retrieved the keys and inserted them into the locked door that read Mayor's Office. The door swung open silently and Penny and Tripp stepped inside, closing the door behind them and leaning on it heavily as they caught their breath.

"That was fun. I know it's silly to be nervous, but it's so quiet out there," I said.

"I know. I feel like I'm really breaking into a building." Tripp smiled at me.

I took a long look around the room. The mayor's desk was a rich cherrywood with a matching chair tucked in behind it. An American flag stood to the left by the wall. Centered on the wall behind the desk was a huge drawing of the original map of the city. You could see which streets still existed and which neighborhoods were part of the original design. Windows ran along the outside wall, but the shades were all drawn.

"Where do we look first?" Tripp asked.

"Well, it's your dad's office, you should know," I said with a cocky grin.

"Ah, if only I actually had that information. I guess we'll just have to rely on Beth's sixteen books worth of previous experience and women's intuition." He took a step closer to me, crowding my space. He smelled good, masculine, but I couldn't help but wonder if I was actually smelling him, or Steve. He put his hands on my waist. "Is this a good time to go off-script?"

So, we spent a couple minutes getting familiar with each other, stopping when Tripp backed me into one of the wingback guest chairs that faced the mayor's desk. I gracefully (like a baby giraffe) fell over the arm and into the seat. Tripp, less than gracefully, followed me down, turning his body at the last minute so he landed on the floor rather than crushing me. He popped back up after barely touching the floor, I admired his agility. Laughing, he grabbed my hand and helped me out of my awkward position in the chair. As I stood, I noticed a portrait on a wall otherwise covered in bookcases.

"This is probably a cliché, but let's see if there's a safe behind the picture of the old guy." I pointed it out.

Tripp walked over to the wall and gently lifted the frame. It swung open like a door to reveal a safe in the wall behind.

"That was too easy." He pulled out the ring of keys again and selected one that was too small to be a door key. He grumbled, "So the town's most important documents include a twenty-five-year-old copy of the contents of a high school time capsule? I have issue with the believability of this plot line." The safe door, of course, opened easily.

I giggled as he pulled out several manila folders and envelopes.

"Oh, look!" Tripp said sarcastically. "Why, it's a list of items included in the time capsule. What a surprise," he deadpanned.

I took the envelope from him and opened it. I pulled out a thin sheaf of typewritten papers. I skimmed the first page; it just told about the time capsule, where it was kept, and when it was to be opened. The next two pages were a basic list of the contents, most of which we knew. The last page was a list of all the senior class members who had contributed items. I ran my finger down the names.

"Both the principal and librarian put notes in the capsule. Nothing from Mr. Louie. He was younger, so

I'm not surprised. I think this is all we were supposed to discover during this scene."

"This was a pretty basic scene. Was the list supposed to have been a big reveal? I feel like we're missing something." Tripp frowned.

I pondered a second. "If we were really Steve and Beth, this little excursion would have been laced with worry about getting caught. And, I think maybe it helped us eliminate Mr. Louie. Bobbie didn't really say anything other than go to city hall and look at the list."

"Okay. Check. Let's head out. I don't suppose I have to bother putting everything back. It's not like anyone is going to come behind us and raise an alarm."

"No, I don't suppose." I set the envelope and papers back in the safe anyway.

We made to leave the office, Tripp placed his hand at the small of my back and reached ahead to open the door for me. As I stepped through, a loud slam echoed through the building, and we heard shoes on marble tapping in our direction.

"Shoot!" I shoved back into Tripp closing us behind the office door.

"What was that? I thought no one was supposed to be here."

"I think Bobbie may have omitted a few plot points to help spice up our date." My heart was racing.

"Be logical. This is what would have made the scene suspenseful for Steve and Beth. They were either caught or they weren't. If we sneak out now and don't get caught, the scene can end. If we get out and don't get sent back, then we know we were supposed to get caught. We'll have to go back inside and face the music," Tripp reasoned.

He was right, I just needed to think about how all this worked with my rational brain. "If we aren't meant to get caught, it won't matter what we do. We can dance right by whoever that is and if it's not scripted, they won't even notice us."

"But before we go, I wanted to talk to you about my sister. How is that going to work?"

"Are you sure you're ready to expose that part of your life to me?" So far, I knew very little. He was tight-lipped about everything but the basics. I didn't even know his last name for goodness sakes.

"I think so. She's pretty insistent, so it's let her in, or I deal with her nagging."

"Well, the only scenes left are the big reveal, the dance, and the game." I ticked each item off on my fingers.

"If the reveal is next, shouldn't we actually know who done it?"

"Crud, probably. Okay, we eliminated Mr. Louie and the Cavaliers. That leaves us with Ms. Frank and Principal Dunn. Which one?" I asked.

"The muddy shoe print. It was too small to be Dunn's."

"Excellent! It was Ms. Frank in the library with the time capsule." I put my hand up for a high five, but Tripp grabbed it and kissed the back instead.

"So do you want Kaitlyn there for the reveal, or wait until the dance?"

"Let me talk to Bobbie, she'll know which scene we can add extra characters to. I'll text you and we can work out a time. Do you want to say tentatively Sunday night? I know you said Saturdays are busy at your store."

"That sounds good. We can text out the rest of the details. Ready to go?"

"Sure."

Tripp eased the door open, and again we heard a door slam and footsteps. This time, he pulled me behind him as we eased the door shut and headed back across the lobby. Unfortunately, it sounded like the other intruder was coming down the same corridor we were headed for. Tripp hurried us over to the hall door and gently pushed me flat against the wall.

The door next to us opened and a man somewhere between forty-five and sixty wearing a business suit came through and continued across the lobby. About midway, he stopped and looked over at the reception desk as if he'd heard something. He started walking toward it, when a car horn sounded from the street out front. The man looked at his watch, then continued toward the front entrance, forgetting about whatever he'd heard behind the desk.

We watched in silence as he exited the building, locking the front door behind him. When he was gone, I sat down and started giggling. Tripp just watched me with mild amusement.

"I guess we should have hidden behind the desk," Tripp said, causing me to laugh harder. I had no idea why, it really hadn't been funny. What was funny was my whole entire life and this whole scenario, and Tripp, who had stopped questioning and gamely played along with the utter ridiculousness of the situation. If nothing else, that alone was enough reason to love this guy. I pulled myself together and Tripp helped me to my feet.

"Was that your dad?"

"I have no idea." Tripp was fully smiling now; it was a beautiful smile. He hadn't graced me with its full force very often. "Let's get out of here."

We escaped out the back door and ran into the adjacent park, panting and laughing at our supposed close call. Tripp stopped, finally, and pulled me in for a hug. He cupped the back of my head and nuzzled my hair near my ear.

"You'll text me tomorrow?" he mumbled.

"Um hmm," I responded, enjoying the closeness. Agreeing to share this with his sister seemed to ease his apprehension. He behaved differently with me; he was more open. I loved it. "I have one question about Kaitlyn, though."

He pulled his head back. "What is it?"

"Do you think she'll like me?"

"Ah, Pen. How could she not?"

Chapter 16

Short and Too Sweet

Bobbie and I opened together Saturday morning. I slept well after my little adventure with Tripp, even though we were done by seven o'clock—the same time we started. Regardless, our book excursion had been suspense-filled and emotional; it exhausted me. After a good night's rest, I prepared to interrogate Bobbie about the information she left out of read-in prep. I know I told her not to give away plot points, but I could have used a warning about almost being caught by a random character. I arrived downstairs just as she was letting herself in.

"Good morning! You're up early." She greeted me as she relocked the shop door behind her.

"I slept well after all the excitement last night." I prepped the coffee maker. I may have been awake, but I couldn't qualify as a functioning human without my joe.

"Do tell. Did you make any headway with Tripp?" Bobbie stashed her purse behind the counter and began readying the sales desk for duty.

"Well, there was more kissing than usual. He told his sister about me, and I think he's passed some kind of internal hurdle. He was different last night, in a good way. But you might have mentioned the other character in the scene. It scared me to death. You said it would be just Tripp and I."

"Pfft! It was nothing. If you were supposed to get caught, I would have warned you about it. A little adrenaline jump never hurt anyone. Did you find out anything useful about our mystery man?"

"Like I said, he told his sister about me, and the whole thing, actually."

"Really?" Bobbie stopped working and gave me her full attention. "What did she say? Does she think he's crazy?"

"She wants to come with him. I don't know if she totally believed him, but at least she's open to being convinced. Boy, is she in for a shock." I laughed. "So, O oracle, when would be a good time for Tripp to read us in?"

Bobbie thought for a minute. "There are only the three scenes left: the Scooby-Doo-style reveal, the homecoming dance, and the big game. You don't want his sister in for the reveal. She might end up being one of the major players, probably Ms. Frank, and throw everything off. It would just be confusing for her."

"She'd probably like the dance."

Bobbie gave me a sheepish look. "She might…but I kind of promised Biddy she could come. She was looking for a lark and misses the read-ins she used to do with your gram. I figured she could do the least harm at the dance, and I really don't want to expose a brand new person to Biddy. You never know what she might say."

"True that!" I agreed whole-heartedly. "That leaves the game."

"That'll be our best bet. She'll most likely come in as another one of the cheerleaders. We'll be able to corral her and get her acclimated without causing too much disruption."

"Okay, I'll let Tripp know. We can set a tentative read-in date for, gosh, next weekend maybe?" The time had zipped by, but Tripp didn't seem anywhere close to being ready to meet in person.

"Coming right up. You've got some headway to make, girl, otherwise we'll have to start thinking about the next book. I recently read this great paranormal romance, not my usual taste, but you'd like it—"

"We"—I quickly interrupted—"can talk about that another time." I sent a quick text to Tripp, which reminded me I still needed to ask him about his California area code. It was eight thirty, which would make it five thirty Cali time.

—*Hope this isn't too early to text. Sorry if I woke you.*—

—*Why? I'm up.*—

—*Your area code is CA. It's still pretty early there.*—

I've had this number since I was stationed there several years ago.—

—*Oh.*— Dang it! Stumped again.

—*What's up?*—

—*Read-in tomorrow night? Three scenes left. Bobbie said your sister can come to the last one. Possibly Sat night.*—

—*Okay. What time tomorrow?*—

—*Seven? East Stand time.*—

—*Same as me. (-; See you then.*—

"Woop!" I yelled and fist-pumped the air.

Bobbie fumbled her cleaning rag at my shout. "What?"

"He lives on the East Coast. Somewhere." Still not much information, but I couldn't help smiling. I felt like I'd actually learned something real. "That means he's potentially within driving distance."

"Why the California phone number?" Bobbie resumed wiping down the countertops.

"He was stationed there. Remember he mentioned he'd been in the marines?" And then quickly changed the subject, I now recalled. He didn't like to share much, but that topic seemed particularly private.

"Right. Be sure to add that tidbit to your list of Tripp information, short though it may be," she advised.

"Are you and Peter coming to the reveal read-in tomorrow night?" I reached for the notebook containing my Tripp list.

"We wouldn't miss it. It's the culmination of all my hard manipulating, after all—my reward for not only having to read through that insipid book, but then also living through some of it."

****

After a quick take-out dinner Sunday night, Bobbie, Peter, and I once again congregated in the reading nook toward the back of my shop. I had my book and they were settled in with fresh cups of coffee, which I decided to forgo, since I was already a little keyed up.

"I'm so excited, I can't believe it's already time for the reveal. You know, I always wanted to be Daphne." I referred to my favorite Scooby-Doo character—not that there were many options for favorite girls.

"So, you figured out who stole the capsule?" Peter asked.

"Yes, the librarian. Right?" I looked at Bobbie, who nodded.

"But did you come up with a motive?" she asked.

I frowned. "No, I was kind of busy with my own mystery, thank you very much. Was I supposed to?" And kissing. We had also been busy with kissing.

Bobbie shrugged. "No, not necessarily, I get that your concentration was divided. Beth and Steve didn't come up with motive either. It will all be made clear in the reveal," she said with dramatic flourish.

"Whatever. Are you guys ready?" When they both nodded affirmative, I double checked the time and began reading.

Pom Squad Mystery #17
"You're probably wondering why I asked you all to meet me here this morning," Beth said as she gazed at the crowd assembled in the school library. The scene of the crime, as it were. The only person actually invited was Principal Dunn. Everyone else was in the library anyway. The assemblage looked toward the circulation desk, though, as Beth made her announcement.

"Beth, you're such a fine student, I certainly don't mind giving you a moment of my time," Principal Dunn said indulgently.

"As you know, I have a bit of a reputation for solving mysteries," Beth continued, smiling at Steve and her other friends who were there to lend their support. "I, along with my friends, have been looking into the problem of the missing time capsule. After weighing all the evidence, we have concluded that you, Ms. Frank, are the guilty party," Beth said, turning to look at the stunned librarian.

Ms. Frank's face turned bright red.

"Is this true, Eloise?" Principal Dunn asked doubtfully, but Beth spoke up to answer.

"We discovered a woman's boot print in the fresh mud on the sidewalk left by the faulty sprinklers. There were no signs of forced entry, leading us to know the culprit must have had a key. We caught Cavaliers attempting to steal the Warrior pelt from the gym, which they would not have attempted if they already had the capsule in their possession. And finally, the only people with possible motives are members of the graduating class of 1933, of which you, Principal Dunn, and Ms. Frank were both members. You, of course, are eliminated due to wearing size thirteen men's shoes. The only thing I don't know is why," Penny said. Tripp had moved close enough to reach her hand and gave it a squeeze.

Ms. Frank sobbed. "I was just so embarrassed! In twenty-five years, I'd planned to be married." She cast a longing look at Dunn. "And be a famous author. I wrote all about it in that silly letter and sealed it up in the time capsule. Nothing worked out as planned; I'm so ashamed!" She buried her face in her hands, her shoulders shaking in silent anguish.

Principal Dunn looked astonished. "I thought you were happy here as the school librarian."

"Oh, I am, but I had hoped to be married."

"Why did you never marry?" Dunn asked quietly.

Ms. Frank peeked at him through her fingers. "The love of my life went off to college and forgot about me."

"I never forgot about you," Dunn said, peeling her hands away from her face.

"You never wrote!" she replied shortly.

"This is a freaking soap opera," Tripp whispered.

"Shhh, it's romantic," I said, but saw Bobbie making a gagging gesture over Tripp's shoulder.

"I was embarrassed. You were always so much smarter than I was. You got accepted to a better school. I didn't want to hold you back." The weight of all the wasted years suddenly visible in his eyes.

Ms. Frank pulled her key from her desk drawer and turned to a corner cabinet. "Here's the time capsule," she said, unlocking the door. "I'm sorry." She too, looked sad and defeated.

Mr. Dunn gently took the capsule from her. Clearing his throat, he said, "All's well that ends well. It's been found in time for the homecoming celebration, so no harm done. Thank you, Beth, and friends, for your efforts in recovering this important piece of our upcoming festivities."

"Um, sure thing," I said.

Dunn continued, "I think it's best that we all move forward from here and look to a bright and hopeful tomorrow."

I rolled my eyes. Maybe Bobbie was right about how bad these books were. From the back of the room, a kid with a crew cut threw a hand in the air.

"But Mr. Dunn, what are we going to do about a basketball coach?" he asked.

Bobbie stepped up and whispered to me. "This is your line, but I'm going to cover it for you." Then said, "I have a suggestion I think you'll love."

****

And then we were back in the bookstore.

"What?! That's it? I didn't even get a chance to talk to Tripp." Or kiss him, for that matter.

117

"Sorry." Bobbie shrugged "When these books wrap up, they wrap up fast."

"I didn't even get to do anything," Peter grumbled. Bobbie patted his knee.

"We still have the dance, which I'll enjoy, and the game, which I know you and Tripp will look forward to."

"It was still lame. You could have warned me it would go that fast." I pulled out my phone to text Tripp an apology for the shortness and hokey-ness of our jaunt.

Chapter 17

Enough with the Revelations Already

I was still a little sore at Bobbie for her nondisclosure regarding our last read-in. As punishment, I decided to work on my genealogy project upstairs in my apartment rather than hang out in the store while she worked her shift. Of course, Bobbie didn't realize it was punishment. It was mostly me saving myself the aggravation of having her constantly looking over my shoulder while I went about my research in the most disorganized way possible. Hey, that's just the way I work, which drives her nuts, then she, in turn drives me nuts about it. I basically cut out the middleman, because I was perfectly capable of driving myself nuts all on my own. Did I mention how thoroughly I abhorred research?

I was pleased, though, to open up my email and find a response from the Smithton Historical Society. A woman named Jeanie Harden was thrilled with my interest. She attached ten different documents to the email and provided an address, should I want to make a donation. Though there were no longer any members of the Grant, Freeman, or Franklin families living in Smithton, she sent me the information she had found. As a small community, she explained, most of the families had opportunity to make a name for themselves locally, be it at the local fair or by being involved in school or church. They had a small newspaper, and things that would seem mundane to city folk were often front-page news. I hoped what she sent me proved to be more exciting than a blue-ribbon jar of jelly.

The first attachment was an enrollment list from Smithton Consolidated School dated 1860. Jeanie noted for me that Abigail Grant and Hazel Franklin were both in the first grade. Next, was a birth announcement and birth certificate for Dolores Freeman in 1874. Her parents were listed as Abigail Grant Freeman and Haden Freeman. There was a marriage announcement for Hazel Franklin and Albert Archer in 1876, an 1885 birth announcement for John Archer, and a marriage certificate for John and Mary Archer.

Some of the documents held little interest for me. I didn't really care about what committees anyone was on, but I appreciated Jeanie's thoroughness. The last document of interest was a marriage announcement for Dolores Freeman to Edward McKay of Upper Orrington. This search led directly to my backyard. I wracked my brain to recall having gone to school with any McKays. It was a possibility.

I quickly sent a reply to Jeanie, thanking her for her diligence and telling her how helpful the information had been. I jotted down the address so I could send them a check when I next paid bills. Then I organized all my new information into a timeline of sorts. After that I played solitaire on my laptop until I could reasonably consider it lunch time-ish. I made peace pb&js and brought one down to Bobbie—not that she even knew I'd been irritated and needed to make amends, but still.

"Mmm, crunchy peanut butter, my favorite." Bobbie peeked between her bread slices. "To what do I owe this treat?"

"Just celebrating a successful research morning. I actually didn't have to do much. The Smithton Historical Society really came through. I spent most of the time looking through and organizing the information they sent." I munched on my own sandwich. I showed Bobbie the updated Cleary family timeline.

She clicked through the documents on my laptop. "So you're looking for a McKay now? Here, in Upper Orrington?"

"Looks like. I'm getting close. It's pretty exciting." I took another bite of my sandwich.

But Bobbie was ignoring me now. I could see the wheels turning.

"Wasn't your neighbor's last name McKay? Gregorio's uncle?"

Mind like a steel trap, that girl. Holy crap, she was right!

"Holy crap! Gregory McKay. No way is that a coincidence." My mind flew through the possible ramifications. "Gregorio could be the one?" I suggested, then dismissed. "Or Gregorio could be the father or grandfather of the one. Creepy."

"And," Bobbie cut in, "you and Gregorio share common ancestors, Elizabeth and Danior."

"No. Freaking. Way."

"That is, if these McKays are the same as Gregorio's McKays. You're a couple of generations short of being sure."

I stuffed the rest of my sandwich in my mouth, grabbed my paperwork, and ran back upstairs. I easily found the obituary online for Gregorio's uncle from a few months back. He was the oldest of three; Gregory, Sylvia, and Patricia McKay. His parents were James and Lucille.

I could probably get my questions answered with a really awkward phone call to Gregorio's mom; I doubted Gregorio would know his family history that far back. But I wasn't ready to have to explain myself to Gregorio (whom I would need to ask for his mom's number), nor his mom. Why would some random girl be interested in Gregorio's great, great, greats? I'd have to see what I could find on my own first.

Since Mr. McKay's obituary was so helpful in giving me his parents' names, I used the Upper Orrington Press archives to see if I could find an obit for James. I was not disappointed. Rather quickly, I found an obituary and a nice article about James McKay and his contributions to the Upper Orrington business district development, of which my little shop was a part. James's father was Edward McKay Junior. Bingo. I didn't feel the need to go any further. Sure, I could dig up a birth certificate that said my Edward Senior and Dolores were Edward Junior's parents, but this town is just not that big, and it was even smaller at the end of the nineteenth century. I was certain I had my man. And Gregorio was my cousin, a jillion times removed.

Chapter 18

You Can Dance

"I really need to be able to talk to him this time," I told Bobbie as she stood at the counter preparing coffee for herself and Peter and tea for Biddy.

"I know, you've only told me about thirty times." She handed me the tea so I could deliver it to Peter's grandmother. Biddy was decked out in her Sunday best, complete with gloves and rose corsage. She had book walked with my gram in the past, so she knew the ropes. I had no idea why she bothered to dress the part, I, myself wore sweatpants and t-shirt. I had discovered that Biddy had reached an age where she pretty much does what she wants. I wasn't going to question it— at least not out loud.

Bobbie joined us in the bookshop reading nook and handed Peter his coffee. "If you want to talk to Tripp you need to pull him aside right when we get there. Otherwise, things will start rolling and you might not get a chance."

"What do we do while they're off talking?" Peter asked.

"We will be dancing. This is a date. Surprise!" Bobbie took her seat, ignoring Peter's appalled expression.

"Close your mouth, Petey. You'll catch flies. If you'd take this girl on a proper date once in a while she wouldn't have to resort to trickery," Biddy scolded.

"I take her out all the time," Peter protested.

"And as much as I enjoy a good basketball game or three, or baseball, or hockey, I like to do girly things once in a while, too. Besides, Penny needs our support."

I totally did not need help at this point, but I wasn't about to contradict Bobbie and ruin her date. Weren't Tripp and I essentially doing the same thing? Except that these read-ins were the only dates we ever went on. Maybe I should resort to some of my own trickery.

I sent Tripp a quick text. He said he should be able to get away from the sales floor for a minute, because no matter how long we were actually gone, no time was lost in real life. I wanted to make sure he was still good to go.

—*All set?*—

—*Yep. C U soon.*— Tripp texted back immediately.

"We're good to go, everybody." I opened my book up to the second to last chapter.

Pom Squad Mystery #17

Beth felt the snap of the ruler all the way through Steve's hand. It must have smarted, but he obediently moved his hand back to her waist from where it had strayed to her hip.

"And one foot apart, Mr. Simpson," Mrs. Fitzgerald said as she thrust her ruler between the teens.

Beth stepped back so that her fingers barely grazed Steve's shoulders. The diligent chaperone nodded her head in approval before moving on. She took a few steps, then turned and spoke.

"If you want to have time to talk, you'd best be about it. Nice to see you again, Tripp," Biddy said. "I'd hoped to be a pretty young thing with a hot date…maybe I can get Petey to dance one with me." She hurried off.

Even with the dated haircut, Tripp was devastatingly handsome in his suit, and when he grinned at me, oh my, was it warm in here?

"A friend of yours?" he asked.

"That's Peter's grandmother, Biddy. She used to book walk with my grandmother back in the day. Bobbie promised she could come. You met her the first time we met, back in Margrave," I explained.

"I don't remember, but she seems wise. Let's get out of here." He grabbed my hand and started heading toward the double doors leading into the school. I struggled to keep up with his stride in my pinchy heels.

The double doors swung closed behind us, effectively cutting off all sound from the party beyond. Tripp immediately spun me into his arms and greeted me with a hello kiss.

"You look beautiful," he said when he finally released me.

I took note for the first time of what I was wearing. So. Much. Tulle. My dress was all poufy pink tulle, yards of the stuff. It crisscrossed my chest and swooped over my shoulders. The skirt was tea length and I think I had on some sort of crinoline to make it stick out even more. The torturous little shoes were, of course, dyed to match.

Tripp, on the other hand, was perfect. Pressed black slacks, crisp white shirt and jacket, sharp black bowtie. He was somewhere between sexy waiter and James Bond. Also, he smelled delicious. Like forest and aftershave with a bit of something I couldn't identify.

"Thanks. So do you. Look good, I mean," I stumbled out. "I'm sorry we didn't get to talk last time. I didn't know it would be so quick."

"No big deal. We've got tonight. Are your friends here too?"

"Yes, Bobbie's making Peter take her to the dance as a date." I smiled.

"Good, so we don't need to rush." Tripp leaned in to kiss me again.

Reluctantly, I put my hand up to stop him. "No, but we do need to talk. Preferably somewhere we can sit."

Tripp led me down the hall a bit farther to where there were benches lining the walls. He settled me into a corner, then sat and pulled my feet onto his lap where he proceeded to remove my shoes and do wondrous things to my aching feet. "What do we need to talk about?"

I tried to concentrate. "Well, there's only one chapter left after this. We need to decide if we're ready to meet or if we need to do another book. If we do another book, which one?"

Tripp continued to rub while he contemplated my question. "I need more time. Maybe not an entire book, but more. If you don't start another one, I won't see you." He seemed genuinely sad at the idea.

I put a finger on his chin and tipped his head to look at me. "It's okay. You can have more time."

He switched to start on my other foot. "What book do you want to read?"

"Well, my criteria for last time was no sex." I blushed. He was looking down at my feet, but I caught sight of his dimple. "And an opportunity to talk. This book has been pretty tame, but it provided both of those things. Bobbie and I hadn't figured out how everything worked yet, so we were playing it safe. We, of course, now know that we can go off script at any time to talk. Now that you've self-realized, we can choose to skip any bits of plot we're not comfortable with. I mean, I still don't think we should pick a torrid bodice-ripper for next time, but I think we could handle an adult novel."

He looked at me, one eyebrow cocked up. "You mean there were circumstances where sex wasn't a choice?"

"Let's just say one of my grandmothers found herself in a situation where she was thoroughly persuaded that it was the right choice. She's the one who always referred to the legacy as a curse in her letters."

"I can't wait to hear that story."

"Mmm," I agreed. "Anyway, since I chose this book, I thought you might have an opinion about the next one."

"Not particularly."

"I don't want to pick something you'll hate. I was thinking John Grisham, but it might end up being dangerous." I shrugged. I was at a loss.

"Something active."

"What?" I found it hard to focus while my feet were in ecstasy.

"How about something active? I liked the basketball in this one."

"So, a sports novel?" I struggled to hide my disappointment.

"Not necessarily. It can be an outdoor adventure or something."

I wrinkled my nose. "Outdoor adventure sounds like something that will find us in peril. I am not interested in being tossed about in a river or chased by a grizzly."

"Not an outdoors girl then, are you?"

"I like camping well enough, but the only camping novels I can think of off-hand take place at Camp Crystal Lake. No, thank you." Tripp had the nerve to laugh at me. "I really hate to even suggest this, but I promised Bobbie I would ask you. She keeps suggesting some paranormal romance book she's just read."

"I don't know Bobbie very well, but that doesn't sound like her normal reading material."

"Oh trust me, it's not. I think she has a morbid curiosity to see how the paranormal stuff plays out when we book walk."

He eyed me nervously. "I'm afraid to ask, but what would my character be?"

"A vampire."

"And yours?"

"I think she said I'd be a human that falls in love with you." I cringed; I would totally get off easy on this one.

"And what else should I know about this book?" He stopped rubbing my feet to look me in the eye.

I half smiled. "There are also werewolves."

"Oh no, I am not going to be some sparkly—"

I put my hand on his chest before he got too riled. "It's not that book. I promise, no sparkling, no love triangle. I'll check with Bobbie about how 'active' it is for you. How do you even know about that series anyway? It doesn't sound like your preferred reading material either. Or any self-respecting guy, really."

"Kaitlyn read the series back when it came out, then made me take her to see the movies. All of them. It was torture. You'll need to let me know the title, so I can pick up a copy. Kaitlyn won't want to miss it."

"Okay. That's settled, sort of. The next thing is a list of things you need to tell Kaitlyn before she comes with you next time. It's from Bobbie. She's an over-planner."

"It's fine. I got that impression." He finished with my feet and gently replaced my shoes. With them still on his lap, he slowly traced circles on one ankle as we talked. It was pleasantly distracting.

"Just explain about going off-script. And that all the regular characters will keep doing their own thing, so she shouldn't worry about messing anything up. Bobbie and Peter will both be there, but Bobbie said that the Warriors win the game and that's the end, so there won't really be time for formal introductions. Kaitlyn will most likely show up as one of the cheerleaders, so Bobbie and I can snag her and answer questions while you and Peter tear up the court again."

"I'm looking forward to that. I just wish it wasn't so easy; there's no challenge. Maybe I can get Peter to play one on one with me instead."

"Well, whatever. Just make sure Kaitlyn is prepped. I'm sure it will all work out. Are you ready to head back to the dance?"

"Are your feet going to be okay?"

"If they get too sore, I'll just go barefoot. Who's going to say anything?" I winked at him.

"Let's go, then." This time Tripp offered me his arm and escorted me back through the double doors.

The music was playing, and couples were swaying on the dance floor. I spotted Bobbie and Peter right away, they'd probably been waiting for us. Peter was decked out similarly to Steve. Well, actually, identically to Steve, as was every other guy on the floor. Bobbie evidently got the long straw dress-wise. Hers was all baby blue Chantilly lace with cute cuff sleeves. She was probably also wearing a poufy crinoline underneath, but it didn't make her look like cotton candy as it did yours truly.

"This is so much fun!" she said, giving me a hug. "Have you seen your hair?"

My hand immediately reached for the top of my head, and kept going, as the top was a couple inches taller than usual. I made a note to avoid mirrors. The dress was bad enough, I didn't need to also be self-conscious about a crazy up-do as well. Bobbie's hair curled under and she wore a cute little headband that matched her dress. Her shoes, I also noted, were discreet flats. Where do the rules say the main character has to be the fanciest? I completely envied Bobbie's wardrobe even though I was supposedly better outfitted.

I also noticed Biddy had abandoned her chaperoning duties and circled the dance floor with one of the regular characters. Huh. I didn't realize you could force them off script too. Though he's probably scripted to be dancing with somebody. I wondered where his date went.

"Did you give him instructions for his sister?" Bobbie asked, drawing my attention away from the dancers.

"Yes, she'll be ready. And we discussed the next book, too."

"And? Is he willing to do the paranormal romance?" She was practically salivating.

Peter and Tripp said their hellos and excused themselves to go get punch for us all. I'm not sure what he would have made of Bobbie's excitement over the vampire book. It made me nervous, but I trusted her.

"Conditionally. He wants a book that's active; like the basketball in this story, but not necessarily a sports novel. Do the vampires run around some?" I had a sudden hilarious image of vampires running around in circles with their teeth dripping blood and had to stifle a laugh.

"Without giving away too much, I can tell you that there is some escaping that happens, and that's pretty active. Also some supernatural jumping and climbing and such."

"That sounds active, but not sporty, so it will probably be fine. It's not dangerous, is it? Who is he escaping from?"

She paused briefly before answering. "After all is said and done, it's still a romance. The danger is negligible and certainly no worse than Margrave."

I put my hands on my hips and tapped my foot. "That's not really an answer. I seem to remember a terrible horseback ride and near-rape in Margrave as well as the tower incident."

"The tower incident was really your fault. Listen, we can make it perfectly safe, I promise." Bobbie reassured me.

"Fine. I'm sure Tripp will agree."

"I'll agree with what?" Tripp and Peter handed us each a glass of yellow punch, in real glasses.

"Bobbie said the vampire book is active, but now she's trying to convince me it's also safe."

Tripp slung an arm over my shoulder. "Don't worry, I'll keep you safe, when I'm not trying to suck your blood, mwah ha ha!" He leaned in and nipped my ear, nearly earning himself a punch bath. I'll admit, I was enjoying this new lighter side of him, though. Bobbie just rolled her eyes at us.

"I'll have Penny text you the title and author so you can get your own copy. Providing your sister wants to continue to join us after tomorrow night," she said.

Biddy was circling around to our group again. When she reached us, she made her unnecessary apologies to her partner and joined us. "The music is all over the place, dears. When does this book take place?"

"The late 1950s, I believe," I said. "But this one was published in 1965, so the author probably fudged the musical timeline a little."

"That would explain it. When does this show get on the road? I'm pooped." Peter handed her his own, yet-untouched glass of punch. "Petey, you're a doll."

The band finished their set, and there was a loud squeal as Principal Dunn took over and adjusted the microphone on stage.

"Good evening, students, I hope you're enjoying all of the homecoming festivities. First, I want to congratulate the pom squad on the fabulous decorations you see around you. You girls have truly outdone yourselves." He paused while everyone applauded. "I want to remind everyone to come out tomorrow night and show your Warrior Spirit in support of our basketball team. The homecoming game is the biggest of the year. As you know, we'll be playing the La Salle Cavaliers. Let's make sure the stands are filled with Warriors." More applause, then Ms. Frank joined him on stage carrying the time capsule.

"At this time, I'd like to ceremoniously unlock the time capsule. This isn't the time to sort through its contents, but everything will be available for viewing in the coming weeks." He unlocked the capsule, which was no more than a lockbox the size of a large shoe box. He then pulled out the top sheet of paper and read it. "Dear Warriors of 1958, we made it! We've traveled twenty-five years into the future to impart our wisdom on your generation. If you're not too busy with your flying cars and moving sidewalks to hear it, that is. We, the class of 1933, want to tell you to never miss a chance to seize an opportunity. Follow your dreams. If something makes you happy, then it's worth going after. You're Warriors, and Warriors don't believe in fear! Sincerely, The Class of 1933." The gym once again thundered. Principal Dunn finally made settling motions with his hands and the students quieted.

"Ahem. Wise, wise words from the class of 1933. My own graduating class, incidentally." He pulled at his collar nervously. "Funny, how people can be so good at handing out advice, but then be reluctant to recognize and follow good advice when they hear it." He put the letter back in the box and closed the time capsule. He handed it off to another teacher who was waiting in the wings. Ms. Frank started to leave the stage, but he put his hand on her arm to stop her.

"I'd like to think it's never too late to follow your dreams and seize opportunity. It's never too late to listen to good advice." He dropped to one knee and took Ms. Frank's hand in his own. "Eloise, I should have never let you go. If I'm not too late, will you please do me the honor of becoming my wife?" The gym was so silent you could hear a pin drop.

"Oh, Fred! Yes!" she replied. Dunn stood and pulled her into a quick embrace. Ms. Frank beamed out at the crowd, which was once again cheering enthusiastically. She leaned over and whispered something in his ear.

"Students, I've just been reminded that we have one last order of business to conduct tonight before we can resume dancing," Dunn said. Another teacher from the sidelines came forward carrying a sealed envelope and a red velvet pillow holding two crowns. He took the envelope and handed Ms. Frank the pillow, then slowly tore open the envelope and pulled out a folded sheet of paper. The man was a fiend for dramatic effect, apparently. He unfolded the paper and stepped back up to the microphone. "The 1958 homecoming queen and king are... Beth Smart and Steve Simpson!"

The crowd started cheering again and I turned to Bobbie. "I suppose I should have expected this."

She grinned at me. "You are the main character, and you did save the day. Get up there and get your crown."

Tripp didn't look especially surprised. He was good at rolling with the punches. He just waited till I was done talking to Bobbie, then held out his hand so he could lead me up on stage.

Chairs had been pulled to center stage and we were directed to sit. I continued to hold Tripp's hand as matching crowns were placed on our heads.

"Congratulations, Steve and Beth, and thank you for your many contributions to Weatherford High School! Especially recently," he added for our ears only. "King Simpson, please lead your queen in the traditional coronation dance."

Tripp led me off the stage and to the middle of the dance floor where the students had made a circle. He pulled me into his arms and started swaying before the music had even begun.

I relished the strength of his arms around me. The band struck up a familiar tune, reminding me that taking chances can have sweet returns. "You didn't seem surprised."

"I know better than to let anything surprise me where you're concerned."

"Any regrets? Am I, is this, disrupting the plans you had for your life?" I felt his muscles tense slightly, then relax again.

"My plans were already disrupted. This, you, are bringing everything in line for me again. You're unexpected, but not unwanted."

"This isn't just about me and my family legacy. It's just as much about you. Please tell me what you need from me, okay?"

He pulled back so he could look me in the eyes. "I will, I promise. For right now, though, you make me happy. I'm not foolish enough to miss the chance to seize an opportunity."

And then he kissed me.

Chapter 19

Do I?

I woke up Saturday morning thinking about my conversation with Bobbie earlier in the week. Tonight was the last read-in for Pom Squad, and the last time I'd see Tripp in that comfortable setting. When we started a new book, there would be an acclimation period before we could figure out the best time to take things off-script.

I'd told Bobbie about the discoveries I'd made about Gregorio. Her response surprised me at first but gave me some things to think about.

"And how do you feel about that," Bobbie asked when I told her where the Cleary line ended up.

I had come downstairs to help her close up, and we were enjoying the last of the coffee in the reading nook chairs. "It's a pretty creepy coincidence," I hedged, because I still wasn't sure how I should feel about it.

"It's Tripp's 'out' you know." She studied me.

"What do you mean?"

"It's your legacy. You can make the rules. If you want to let Tripp off the hook—if you think he's not going to fall in line, you can tell him you were wrong. If you still have strong feeling for Gregorio you want to pursue...well, you have genealogical evidence that he's your guy, possibly." She shrugged.

"I don't know what you mean. Tripp's been there since the beginning. He's the one."

"I know that, and you know that. Have you mentioned our theory and research to Tripp?"

"I don't think so, at least not in any depth." I still didn't understand what she was getting at.

"You can tell him that you've traced the line to Gregorio. By going with him, you can put an end to the legacy. There's no such thing as coincidence. That the line from one potential bachelor should lead to someone you already know, is no less than fate. You can stop all of this right now, never read-in again, and Tripp would have no way to find you, just like you don't have enough information to find him."

My heart skipped a beat in panic. The thought of not seeing Tripp again, well, I didn't even want to explore that idea. Not only that, but for Bobbie's suggestion to work, I'd have to marry Gregorio. She didn't say it, but it was implied, otherwise I'd never be able to pick up a book again. The legacy was clear, the read-ins would stop when I wore my gram's ring in marriage. But no one, not one of my great-grandmas, save Elizabeth, married someone who wasn't their true love. I didn't think the magic would be very happy about that kind of choice. "But that's not what I want!" I finally blurted out.

"Are you sure? Gregorio's hot. And the way he always says 'Penelope' is panty-melting."

"Yes, I'm absolutely sure. He is hot, and nice, but he's only a friend, no matter what he'd wish otherwise. I had an attraction for Gregorio, but with Tripp it's more than that, it's a connection." I paused, trying to formulate the words I wanted. "My feelings for Tripp feel unfinished. Like, I can tell there's more yet to grow, and

I'm excited about that. I don't have any impression of an end date for the relationship. I'm not explaining this very well. Where is this coming from anyway? I thought you liked Tripp. You were the one cautioning me about getting too close to Gregorio."

"Oh, I really do like him," she said flippantly. "I just wanted to make sure *you* really did, so I was playing devil's advocate. And you needed to take a break from being 'in love' to really dissect your feelings before going too much further."

"So do you really think it means anything, me being distantly related to Gregorio?"

Bobbie tilted her head, weighing the facts. "No. I don't. I think if you were to trace every single rabbit trail branch of the Cleary line down to present day, you'd find you're distantly related to more people than you thought."

"Even you?" I asked with a smile.

"Nah, my ancestors are Czechoslovakian. But who knows, maybe Gregorio's grandson will be the true love of your granddaughter to fulfill the legacy."

We sat quietly for a few moments, thinking about that possibility.

"So, do you think I should share this new information with either of the guys?"

"I think you should be careful what, specifically, you tell each of them, if you decide to share. You don't want Gregorio to read too much into the connection. It's really interesting information, but is it information he really needs? You might save it as an interesting anecdote to share over a couples dinner when you both have been married several years. Or when Tripp can be in the same room with him without wanting to punch him in the face."

"And Tripp?"

"Tricky. You don't want him to get agitated by your connection to Gregorio. I'm sure he'd rather the guy just disappear altogether. And you don't want to bog him down with all the details of your research either. Men can get sensitive if they think you are actively seeking out another guy, no matter how innocent your reasons. I feel like he needs to be a little more invested in the relationship before you rock that particular boat."

"It sounds like you're recommending I don't tell either of them," I concluded.

"Yes, I guess that's exactly what I'm saying. Staying silent hurts no one. Speaking, potentially, could upset more than one apple cart."

Now, I was twelve hours away from the *Pom Squad* finale, so to speak, and had been second-guessing my decision to keep silent all day. The shop kept me physically occupied, but my mind was free to run amuck.

I was also nervous about the read-in and meeting Tripp's sister. It being his first on-purpose read-in, I wondered if he was apprehensive too. Probably not. Tripp wasn't, by nature, a nervous guy. We were compatible in that way, I supposed. It wouldn't do for us both to be senseless worriers.

****

"It's almost time, is everyone ready?" I fidgeted with the book in my hands. My anxiety only worsened as the day wore on. I was a complete basket case now.

"We've got ten minutes. I sense Tripp is a punctual guy; he won't pull us in early. Just relax." Bobbie piddled around the shop, and Peter took a quick bathroom break.

I was in a near state of panic, worrying they wouldn't be seated when we started. Oh, I know we don't lose any time, but I felt we should all be seated and ready to go.

"I'm ready." Peter hopped over the back of the chair and plopped into it.

"Peter! The furniture. Biddy would have skinned you," Bobbie scolded.

"Sorry, Pen," he said sheepishly.

"You'll be able to jump and tear around in a few minutes. Try to treat the chairs like you don't own them." Bobbie entered the nook area and settled into the seat across from me. She smiled reassuringly, but it did nothing to calm my nerves. She looked at her watch. "Should be any minute now. I'm interested to see what it's like doing it this way."

With summer right around the corner, it wasn't yet dark outside, but we rarely had after-hours shoppers outside of tourist season. I would have to think about extending my hours next month when evening foot traffic increased.

I could see the sidewalk from where I was sitting, but we were far enough back in the store to require lamps to see properly. This might have led a passer-by to think we were open, or a friend to think we were available for conversation. Such was the case at that moment when Gregorio came walking up the sidewalk from next door and knocked on the window. I knew he could see me, because of the confused look he gave in response to the terror and shock on my face.

Bobbie spun around in her chair. "Shit!" Yes, that about summed it up.

Chapter 20

Anything But Routine

Pom Squad Mystery #17
This was the squad's defining moment, an original routine, more revolutionary than anything done before. The squad had gotten together the previous evening to shorten their skirts in preparation for this evening's half-time unveiling.

Beth led the girls to the center of the gym, then took her position to the right. Patty, as the slightest squad member, took the center position. Beth called out the commands and led the team through two familiar cheers designed to get the audience excited. Barely glancing at Patty to her left and Sandy to her right, she began the final routine.

In unison, the girls began chanting and clapping, but also maneuvering themselves into position around the gym's center circle so that Beth stood in the very center. She lowered herself into a lunge, her right hip parallel to the floor. Sandy, Dorothy, and Susan, still clapping and chanting, positioned themselves around Beth as spotters as Patty placed her foot on Beth's proffered thigh.

"Just like we practiced," Beth whispered, reaching her arms overhead to grasp Patty's hands as she hoisted herself off the ground.

Putting all her weight on Beth's thigh, she gave a little jump and placed her left saddle shoe on Beth's left shoulder. Sandy and the other girls left-off clapping and had raised their hands to support Patty as she drew her other foot up onto Beth's right shoulder. When Patty was reasonably steady, Beth straightened up, keeping her feet shoulder-width apart, and locked her knees. Patty released Beth's hands and placed them firmly on her hips. Beth quickly moved her own hands to grasp the back of Patty's calves. Only then did the other girls move into their own positions.

Sandy placed her left hand on Beth's shoulder, being careful not to upset her balance, while Dorothy did the same on Beth's left. The girls then each raised their outside leg into position on the shoulders of two girls waiting on their knees. Finally, Susan, the only girl besides Patty who could successfully do a split, lowered herself into position in front of the very first public squad pyramid.

The crowd was silent until the very last line of the girls' chant was delivered, then they went wild. Though Penny did detect a few disapproving looks from several of the older teachers in attendance, the overall response was favorable.

"OMG! Holy ship!" Penny heard from above as the pyramid wavered slightly.

Bobbie and the other girls disassembled themselves and moved in behind Penny to catch Patty.

"Just cross your arms and fall back, we'll catch you, I promise," Bobbie told Patty, who was becoming even more unstable.

Patty managed her dismount, but not near as gracefully as originally scripted. Once down, the girls, save Bobbie, Patty, and I, began a parting chant and started clapping, skipping, and jumping their way back to the sideline. We followed, supporting Patty on either side. When we reached the sideline, Bobbie grabbed a nearby folding chair and deposited Tripp's sister in it.

"Hi! You must be Kaitlyn." I held my hand out to her.

She just continued to look around, completely dazed. "I had no idea. I really didn't believe him, not really."

"I'm Penny," I continued when Kaitlyn limply shook my hand, more out of instinct than actual greeting. At the sound of my name, she snapped into focus.

"Where's Tripp?" She stood up, swaying slightly.

Bobbie put a steadying hand on her shoulder. "He's over in the huddle with the team. We're just going to hang here and watch the game. I'm Bobbie, Penny's friend, and my boyfriend Peter is over with the team as well."

At the mention of the guys, my memory kicked in. I scanned the crowd and the boys in the huddle in alarm. Was Gregorio here? Bobbie noticed my agitation and began scanning the gymnasium as well.

"Over there." She gestured. "With the Cavaliers."

I followed her sightline. "This is not going to be good. Shit."

At my expletive, Kaitlyn tore her gaze away from her brother and looked at me. "What's wrong?"

"Um, we accidently brought my neighbor along for the read-in again," I explained.

"Again? Well, at least it won't be a shock for him."

"He and Tripp don't exactly get along."

"That doesn't sound like Tripp." She eyed me critically.

"WARRIORS! GO, FIGHT, WIN!"

"WE ARE CAVALIERS!"

Both teams broke their huddles. Some of the boys returned to the chairs on the sidelines. Tripp and Peter were among the guys taking to the court, as was Gregorio. Bobbie jumped and waved to capture Peter's attention. When he looked at her, she made a pointing motion to where Gregorio stood on the other half of the court. Peter followed her direction and looked briefly surprised when he noticed Gregorio. He raised his hand in a wave, which Gregorio returned with a smile.

Tripp, who had also been looking in our direction, noticed Gregorio as well. He did not smile and wave. He did, self-consciously, run his hand through what was left of his hair and scowled deeply. Gregorio, apparently, was again cast as greaser Billy. If his hair had started the evening slicked back, rigorous play in the first half had released it from its greasy confines. It curled and waved, and one unruly lock hung down his forehead.

After acknowledging Peter, Gregorio noticed Tripp. His smile remained but turned less friendly as he deliberately lifted his hand and ran his fingers slowly through his hair. Peter, having watched the exchange, turned a concerned look back at Bobbie, who smiled nervously and shrugged. We had our own issues to deal with. The whistle blew, and a Cavalier standing on the side threw the ball to a teammate.

"There's Mr. Louie." Bobbie drew my attention away from the on-court drama. The man stood tall and looked years younger in his coach's uniform. We'd never guessed he was so fit underneath his baggy janitorial clothes.

"Who's Mr. Louie?" Kaitlyn asked, still wide-eyed.

"He's a scripted character. He was a janitor and a suspect in this story. It looks like they made him head coach after the other coach had an unfortunate accident," I explained.

"Yes," Bobbie agreed. "It was a tidy fix to the coach problem as well as elevating the position of a kind, deserving, and qualified man."

"Oh," Kaitlyn said, though she still appeared confused. "What happened to Tripp's hair?"

"We show up looking the part we're cast into," Bobbie said. "This is my hair color, but I wear it long and straight without bangs. She fingered the stiff fringe covering her forehead. "Penny's curls are usually far less tamed than this."

I shook my head. Nothing moved except the two little ringlet pig tails at the base of my neck. Cute, but not really my style. Kaitlyn just nodded, then reached up to pat her own head. She felt around the pins and swirls, obviously trying to form a picture of her head in her head.

"So you have no idea what my brother looks like in real life?" she asked.

"He said he usually wears his hair a little longer, but above his collar."

She nodded thoughtfully, then continued to pepper us with questions, which Bobbie and I attempted to answer while still keeping tabs on what was happening on the court. The game was heating up. This time, it was Tripp and Peter against Gregorio. Peter, being the most skilled, was attempting to play in a way that minimized one-on-one play between the other two men. I was impressed at the limited success he was having.

The three ran the court, avoiding scripted players. The characters couldn't actually be hurt, but none of our guys had it in them to purposefully cause an injury. Whenever Peter had the ball, he retained possession if Tripp and Gregorio were near each other. Tripp and Gregorio were at least only using legitimate reasons to lay hands on each other. The game hadn't yet been reduced to NHL fighting levels.

Gregorio, for his part, kept up pretty well. He didn't strike me as a basketball guy, but he'd obviously spent time at a park court at some time in his life. Other than frequent elbow checks shared between the two rivals, he seemed to be enjoying himself despite being outnumbered.

"I have a question." Kaitlyn's eyes flashed. "Who is that jerk that keeps getting all up in Tripp's face?"

Chapter 21

Defensive Stance

Pom Squad Mystery #17
Steve and Roger huddled with the team and their
new coach, Mr. Louie. Coach L had already taught them
some new tricks, and it had paid off in the first half. The
players broke off to grab some water and watch the pom
squad perform their half-time routine. Beth and the girls
had been working hard on a new, surprise routine, and
Steve couldn't wait to see it.

Roger came and stood beside him to watch as the
girls ran onto the floor. The first two cheers were
familiar, but the third must have been the new one.

"No way!" Roger exclaimed. "Look at Patty.
They're going to put her up on Beth's shoulders."

"That's not Patty," I said. "That's Kaitlyn."

"Who's Kaitlyn?" Peter asked.

"My sister." I watched for the moment when Kaitlyn
realized she wasn't Patty…and there it was. Penny had a
firm hold of her calves, but Kaitlyn flailed slightly. I
tensed, ready to rush in and help should she fall, not that
I'd be able to reach her in time. Luckily, the girls seemed
to have everything in hand, and Kaitlyn reached the floor
safely. Penny and Bobbie then led her to the sideline.

"Hey, let's go." Peter grabbed my arm and pulled
me back into the huddle for Mr. Louie's pep talk.

"Okay, boys. I know how bad you want this win. We're ahead, but now is no time to rest on your laurels. I am honored to have the opportunity to coach such a fine team and couldn't hope to fill Coach Turner's shoes. When you win tonight, I want you to do it in honor of Coach Turner. Make him proud! Okay, go, fight, win on three. One, two, three…"

"WARRIORS! GO, FIGHT, WIN!"

"WE ARE CAVALIERS!" blasted from the other side of the court.

Peter and I took positions on the floor. I didn't know what positions we were playing, but it really didn't matter. My legs vibrated with pent-up energy; I'd been looking forward to tearing up the court with Peter again.

Peter waved at someone; I looked across the court. What the hell was it with that guy?! And why did he get to keep his hair? I ran my hand over my own buzz cut in frustration. Why would Penny bring him, especially knowing it's the last chapter and Kaitlyn was going to be here? It didn't make any sense.

Gregorio noticed me and sneered. This game was going to be more interesting than I'd anticipated. Bring it.

The ref blew the whistle, and I sprang into motion, quickly relieving a Cavalier player of the ball. I started up the court, but noticed Gregorio heading my way in my peripheral. I pivoted, tossed the ball to Peter, and threw an elbow in my rival's direction, feeling satisfied when I connected with a rib. He managed to give me a hard shove before taking off after Peter.

I knew Peter was friendly with the guy, evidenced by the absence of checks between the two; he was working hard to limit contact between Gregorio and I.

Peter was the better player out of all of us and easily manipulated the play. I wasn't yet to the point of dispensing with the game in order to take Gregorio out. Penny would be disappointed, so I settled for trying to make him as uncomfortable as possible. He seemed to have a similar strategy.

When the third quarter ended, I headed straight over to check on Kaitlyn, at least that was the main purpose.

"What is he doing here?" I demanded.

"I'm doing fine, Tripp. Thanks so much for coming to check on me," Kaitlyn said in her snottiest tone.

"Not now, Kait. I can see very well that you're fine. I don't have time to chat right now." I grabbed Penny's arm and pulled her away from the group. "Explain."

"He stopped by the shop a second before you read us in. He was standing outside the door. There wasn't anything we could do about it. Totally not my fault, but I am sorry. I wish you two wouldn't see each other as a threat."

"I'm not threatened." I pulled her flush against my body and lowered my mouth to hers. Short on time, I kept the kiss brief. "He's just a pain I'd rather not have to deal with."

"He's my neighbor for a while longer, I can't tell him when to come and go. He's found a renter, and we should be finished up with all this business." She waved her hand around aimlessly. "Before too much longer, right?" Her eyes searched mine.

"Yes. Not much longer, I promise."

"Bobbie says this book ends with a Warrior win and you and Peter being carried away in triumph. We're not going to have time to visit. Kaitlyn's sweet. She seems to be acclimating well. We can text, or even talk, later tonight."

"Debrief at twenty-one hundred?" I smiled as she worked the time math in her head.

"Yeah, I can probably do nine o'clock," she said with a satisfied smirk. "You'd better head back out there."

Over my shoulder I saw the teams returning to the court. "Apologize to Kaitlyn for me, would you please? Just tell her I'll explain at home." Penny nodded, and I stole one more kiss before heading back to the court.

I gave Peter a half-jesting punch in the arm as I walked by. "You don't need to hog the ball."

He eyed me cautiously. "I'm just trying to avoid bloodshed, dude. This book is rated G, you know."

"Let me play, and I promise not to throw the first punch." I wouldn't start anything, but I'd be sure to finish. The whistle blew before Peter could respond, so I tried to make myself look as harmless as possible. I even held back a dirty look as Gregorio ran by and looked at me warily. He wasn't a bad player, certainly not as good as Peter anyway. Not as good as me either, which I could prove if Peter would pass the damn ball.

Finally! I snatched it out of the air and continued up the court. Suddenly, jerk-off was in my way, blocking my progress.

"Penelope is too good for you, Travis." We were both at a standstill, so I'd have to give up the ball or pass.

"I couldn't agree more, but I'm her choice, aren't I." See I could be agreeable. Where the hell was Peter? I feinted to buy some time.

"Are you? Did she really have a choice?" He crowded into my personal space.

"Well, it wasn't you. No need to be sore about it." There. I tossed the ball to Peter as he ran by. Gregorio only made a half-hearted swipe at it, his gaze still fixed on me.

"It was not me. But she has become a cherished friend, and I would not see her hurt. Is there a reason you won't meet her? You do not strike me as hesitant, generally. It is as if you are hiding something."

"I think Penny is a big girl and you should trust her judgment," I said, as Peter scored down at the far end of the court. Play continued around us. Peter made his way to where we were standing, nervously looking between us.

"Are we gonna play, or do we need to cut out and have a conversation?" Peter shuddered slightly at the thought of giving up a ball game for chit chat.

"We're playing." I dragged my eyes away from Gregorio.

Chapter 22

Power Forward

Pom Squad Mystery #17
"See, he just did it again!" Kaitlyn accused.

I figured it wouldn't do any good to mention that Tripp gave as good as he got. I trusted Peter to handle it if things got out of hand. "I think they're just talking," I said, though even I could tell it wasn't a friendly conversation. "That's Gregorio. He's my neighbor. He stopped by unexpectedly just as Tripp read us in."

"What's his damage anyway?"

I colored slightly. "We sort-of dated very, very briefly."

"He's hot. But the hot ones are always jerks." She attempted to flip her hair off her shoulder before realizing it wasn't that long anymore.

"He's really not. We're just friends now." I felt the need to defend Gregorio. He really was a great guy…for someone else.

"If you say so." She eyed me speculatively, weighing the truth in my statement. I don't know exactly what Tripp told her ahead of time, but she obviously felt he needed backup. So much for me trying to make a good impression. She wasn't ready to trust me on the Gregorio issue.

"Listen," Bobbie cut in, "the game's almost over, so we're about out of time. The Warriors win, then they carry the boys around the gym, we follow and cheer. Or we just stand here and watch the whole thing, which is what I vote for. It was very nice meeting you, Kaitlyn, we truly must do this again."

"Um, sure." Which was really the only response Bobbie's statement allowed for.

I tried to finish up on a friendlier note. "Tripp will explain everything when you get back. He can text or call me if you have any questions he can't answer...or he can give you my number and you can contact me directly." How was that for an olive branch?

The crowd started chanting, "5...4...3...2...1!" The buzzer sounded, signaling the end of the game. The scoreboard flashed the winning score, which of course was completely inaccurate since Tripp, Peter, and Gregorio joined the game. Tripp had only a split second to look back at me and briefly wave before he and Peter were scooped up by their teammates and paraded around the gym as confetti rained down from the stands.

"Gah! I'm glad I don't actually have to wash this out tonight." Bobbie futilely picked confetti out of her hair.

Gregorio, being a Cavalier and free of the hoopla, came over to where we were standing. Bobbie and I greeted him while Kaitlyn gave him the stink-eye.

"Gregorio, this is Tripp's sister Kaitlyn," I said after he had kissed both Bobbie and I on the cheek in greeting.

When Kaitlyn reluctantly offered her hand to shake, Gregorio took it, and bowed over it gallantly. "It is very much my pleasure, Kaitlyn," he said.

Kaitlyn raised her eyebrows at me over his shoulder as if to say, "Is this guy for real?" I just nodded to answer her unasked question. She gave him an assessing look. "Likewise, I'm sure."

By this time, the rest of the cheer squad had abandoned us to follow the celebration, leaving us to cool our heels until we returned to real life.

"Penelope, I must apologize for once again ending up in your story."

"It's not your fault. I didn't realize you'd be back at the shop tonight. I should have warned you. It's no big deal," I said.

"I feel like it was a very big deal to Tripp. He is not very happy with me." He glanced at Kaitlyn, then back at me. I had a feeling he wanted to say more but was reluctant to disparage a guy in front of his sister. "I'll talk to you later," he opted to say instead, which probably wasn't the right thing either, because Kaitlyn's sharp eyes darted between us, looking for a hidden message.

"Later!" Bobbie grabbed Kaitlyn and me and dragged us behind the crowd, which had exited the gym and poured into the parking lot.

Fireworks were going off overhead. Tripp and Peter had finally given their fans the slip and met us on a grassy island. Bobbie introduced Peter to Kaitlyn, then the couple slipped off to enjoy the light show until they returned home.

"Hey, Kait. I'm sorry I was so short with you earlier." Tripp slung an arm over her shoulders.

"I'm used to it." She smiled. "I'm more shocked about the apology." She gave him a slug on the arm. "You looked real good out there." It seemed like her voice broke at this last.

Tripp gave her a hard look and a message seemed to pass between them. "Thanks. It's been a while since I've had time to play."

Kaitlyn swiped a hand across her face and smiled up at me. "Penny, it was great to meet you. This has all been…very illuminating."

"I'm glad to meet you too. I'm sure we'll be seeing each other again soon." I spared a glance at Tripp who watched us tentatively.

Kaitlyn responded with a noncommittal affirmative, then turned to watch the fireworks herself, giving us some privacy.

"So, I'll guess we'll chat in a little bit?" I said. "And see each other again…soon?"

Tripp put an arm around my waist. "Vampires and werewolves, huh?"

"Bobbie highly recommends it. It's not her usual thing, so it must be good if she says so. She's very discerning," I assured him, hopefully truthfully. I was skeptical myself. If Bobbie wasn't usually a connoisseur of that genre, how could she tell if it was good? Overhead, the fireworks were slowing. We were running out of time. Tripp realized it too.

"Kiss goodnight?" He turned me in his arms.

"Always."

Chapter 23

Debrief

"That. Was. I don't even have a word to describe it, Tripp! You've been doing this for the past couple months? I can't wrap my brain around it." Kaitlyn reached over from where she sat on my recliner and slapped me on the arm. "And it's happening to you, of all people!" she said incredulously. "You don't have a single fanciful bone in your body. It is SO unfair!"

I moved farther down on the sofa, out of reach before she could slap me again. "I didn't ask for it, so give me a break."

"You seem to be enjoying it," she said seriously.

"I am. I like Penny getting to know the real me."

"Is it, though? The real you? *This* is the real you." She gestured at my whole body. "Or do you mean the fun you; the you who doesn't walk around like he has the weight of the world on his shoulders? That could be the real you all the time, too, if you'd let yourself accept. No one else even sees the thing that is holding you back. The biggest obstacle in your life is invisible to everyone else. Don't you get that? We've all said it enough times."

I got up and moved to the kitchen. I didn't want to have this conversation again. "Do you want something to drink?" I opened the fridge. "I've got beer and cola."

"Ew. No." She followed me and rested her elbows on the small peninsula. "You know I'm right."

"I know." My head still buried in the fridge.

"You have to tell her."

"I know that, too." I withdrew, finally settling on a cola, and looked Kaitlyn in the eyes. I despised the sad looks more than anything else, but the look she gave me was one of empathy. I set my bottle down and walked around the counter to hug my sister.

"I love you, Tripp. I'm really happy this super-cool thing is happening to you, you deserve it. I can't form an opinion of Penny yet; there were too many distractions tonight. I know you're a good judge of character, so I'm sure I'll love her." This of course was all muffled since her face was pressed into my shirt.

"That means a lot to me. Thank you, Kait." I released her from the hug.

"So what's next?" She popped the top off my drink and took a swallow. She wrinkled her nose and handed it back to me.

"I guess we're doing some vampire-werewolf thing." I tipped back the bottle, downing almost half of it at once. Magic book basketball was thirsty work, apparently.

"Ooh, I love paranormal romance! Can I come, please?"

"I don't know. I'll have to check it out. You definitely can't come the first time. Besides, won't it be weird for you to be in a romance book with your brother."

"Yeah. Gross. I didn't think of that. Just find out ahead of time when would be a good time. Penny's friend reads ahead, doesn't she?"

"We'll see." I finished off my drink and set the bottle on the counter to rinse and recycle later.

Kaitlyn gave me a pout that ceased working twenty years ago. "Okay. I'm going to head home. I'll see you at dinner tomorrow?"

"Probably. Yes." I followed her to the door and held it as she stepped onto the landing.

She turned to me one last time. "Remember what I said."

"I will. Promise." I crisscrossed my heart with my finger. She nodded, then bounced down the stairs. I glanced at my watch, I had time to stretch and get ready for bed before texting Penny. Maybe I'd call this time. She and Kaitlyn would view that as a step forward.

****

I blinked once, then again. Gregorio still stood outside the shop door, poised to knock, dumbfounded look on his face. Peter sat at my right, slumped in his chair, relaxed as usual. Bobbie stared at me with a look of someone just having dodged a bullet. I think Gregorio's presence threw an unexpected variable into her carefully controlled plan for this read-in.

I got up and walked to the front to let Gregorio in. He looked at his raised fist, as if wondering what he'd intended to do with it, then dropped it to his side.

"Hi!" I opened the door. He just stood there, so I grabbed the front of his shirt and pulled him inside, re-locking the door behind him. "I didn't expect you this evening."

"No kidding," he replied. "I don't think I'll ever get used to that."

"Well, we'll try not to let it happen again. I didn't think you'd be around tonight."

"I hadn't planned to, but I was in the neighborhood and decided to make sure things were ready for the electrician to come on Monday, that way I wouldn't have to make a special trip over tomorrow. Then I saw your lights." He gestured to the lamps. "And figured I'd say hello and let you know about the electrician and that he had his own key."

I led him to the empty chair and gently pushed him into it. Bobbie handed him a glass of water. He nodded his thanks, then guzzled it down. He glanced at Peter.

"Good game," he said. "Thirsty work."

Peter smiled at him, "I know, right? You too. You should come pick up a game with me sometime."

"I would like that." He turned to me. "Penelope, when are you going to meet this Tripp in person?"

I fidgeted a little in my seat. "We haven't planned anything yet, we're still getting to know each other," I said, maybe a little defensively.

"I am worried about you. I feel like he is hiding something. You are a wonderful person. Why would he hesitate to meet you?"

Bobbie, thankfully, answered for me. "You were fortunate enough to meet Penny in person before being introduced to her family's weird legacy. Poor Tripp got thrust into the legacy first. It's understandable that he's being overly cautious."

Gregorio addressed me again. "You don't know where he lives or even his last name, do you?"

"I met his sister. I know about his work and his family. I know he was a marine."

"Ah, yes. The sister. Cute, but prickly, like a little hedgehog. She didn't like me very much." He gave me a wry smile.

"Well, you were trying to rough up her brother," I said.

"You say that like he was completely defenseless. Not so. I may no longer be sweaty from the game, but my ribs still feel a bit bruised." He tenderly poked around on his torso.

"It was her first read-in, and she was meeting us for the first time. I'm sure her first concern was for her brother's physical and mental wellbeing. I'm sure your presence was very confusing to her. Tripp only prepped her to meet me, Bobbie, and Peter."

"Regardless." He dismissed the Kaitlyn conversation. "You have now finished two books, correct? When are you going to meet? If it were me, I surely would not want to wait so long." His gaze was very direct.

"He promised before we finish the next book." That sounded like a lame excuse even to my ears. I looked at the clock over the check-out counter. "I hate to cut this short, guys, but I have a date with my cell phone shortly." Bobbie was already tidying the coffee bar, and Peter pushed himself out of his chair. Gregorio rose as well. He leaned over and kissed me on the cheek.

"I am always here if you need me."

"I know. Thank you." I gave his arm a squeeze. Bobbie and I definitely needed to find him a woman. It was a wonder he was still single.

I ushered everyone out and gave Bobbie a hug, promising to talk to her the next day and tell her how my conversation with Tripp tonight went. I then ran upstairs and rushed through my nighttime routine and jumped into bed. I made sure my notifications were turned on so I'd be sure to hear Tripp's text, then turned on the local news to keep my mind occupied. I nearly jumped out of my skin when my phone rang moments later rather than dinged with a text alert. I shut off the TV and answered on the third ring.

"Hello."

"Penny, hey. I thought I'd just call this time. I'm worn out from the game, oddly enough, and texting seemed like a lot of effort."

"No, it's great. It's good to talk to you. Kind of weird, though I don't know why it should be." I never realized how much I loved his voice.

"Well, it's the first time we've talked and not been face to face," Tripp said.

"Are you okay, about how it went tonight? What did Kaitlyn think of it all?"

"Yeah. It was fun. I could have done without your neighbor being there, but it is what it is. Kaitlyn was pretty excited. She wants to come again. I told her I'd have to see if it'd be convenient."

"Sure. Bobbie will have to let us know."

"What's the next book?"

"I'm actually not sure, but I'll find out so you can buy a copy."

"So, what did Gregorio have to say when you got back?"

I was silent for a second before answering. "He was worried about me. Heh, heh. He seems to think you're hiding some big, bad secret."

Now Tripp was quiet for a beat. "No, nothing big and bad. Kaitlyn also criticized me for being so closed-off, hence the call instead of a text. I'm trying to move forward."

"A zip code would be a step forward," I suggested.

"All in good time. When will I see you again?"

"If Bobbie actually owns the book, I can get it from her tomorrow. If I have to order a copy, it may take a week. But I hope she wouldn't have suggested it if she didn't own a copy."

"Sounds good. I'm beat, so I'm going to say goodnight. Talk tomorrow?"

"Sure, I'll call you," I said. "Night."

"Sweet dreams, Penny."

****

The next morning was beautiful. I met Bobbie and we walked the quarter mile to church. The town was in full spring. Many of the other shops had planters or hanging baskets out on the sidewalk. I'd have to look at doing that for the bookshop.

"I'm glad I decided to keep mum about the whole ancestry discovery. What do you think I should do now? Go back and trace the other Cleary daughters or move on to bachelor number three, the schoolteacher?"

"I'm sure you're tired of Clearys. Why not move on to the next guy and trace his line down as far as you can. If you hit a dead end, switch back over to the Clearys. It's not like you have a deadline on this assignment," Bobbie suggested.

"Ugh!" I groaned. "I wish there was a deadline! Then, at least, there'd be an end date. At this rate I could be chasing descendants for the rest of my life. In fact, I will, because everyone keeps on having babies. Isn't there something else I can leave to my granddaughters? We do have that new information about the soul mate being able to read himself into the same book. That's totally of interest." I grasped at the slim straw.

"They're *your* descendants. Let your conscience be your guide."

I hated when she made me do that. I decided to change the subject. "So, the next book...do you own it, or do I need to buy one? Also, Tripp asked about it. I told him I'd let him know the title today so he can pick one up." Bobbie bit her lip nervously, which was very unlike her. It was giving me an uneasy feeling about this book, even though I trusted her implicitly. "What's wrong?"

"Nothing," she said quickly. "I'm just a little embarrassed, you know it's not my normal genre."

"You liked it enough to recommend it for me."

"Oh, I really did like it, really. Besides, you really wouldn't want to be part of anything I normally read. I thought it was important to choose something at least one of us was familiar with. Let's just call it a guilty pleasure. Right now, I'm a little hung up on the guilty part, that's all. It's called *Chase the Night*. I have a copy you can use. Tripp will have to order his from Amazon. He won't be able to get it in a store since it's indie published."

"What?" I stared at her blankly.

"What, what?"

"What is indie published?"

"We have our work cut out if we're going to make you a proper bookstore owner, jeez! Indie is short slang for independently published, meaning the author paid to have it published his or herself rather than sending it in to publishing houses and risking rejection. Though there are lots of reasons for authors to go that route. I can't say for sure what her reason actually is. Anyway, Amazon can do it, then you can sell your book through them as well."

"Okay, even though my brain is screaming caution, I trust you, and I know you wouldn't steer me wrong."

She gave me a pained smile. "Never. Besides, it's only a couple weeks out of your life, *and,* if you hate it, just stop reading and go meet in person. The end, right?"

"Right. Either way, this next book is the end."

The End for now.

An excerpt from Book 3 in the *In for A Penny* series:
In for a Penny: A Partially Paranormal Romance

Chapter 1

Fang it!

"Here it is!" Bobbie said, presenting us with the third and hopefully final book in my family legacy fulfillment quest. The legacy that dumped me into the plot of whatever book I happened to read in order to meet my supposed true love.

Chase the Night was an indie-published paranormal romance that Bobbie highly recommended. Since I wasn't currently able to do any recreational reading myself, I had to take her word for it. She was pretty picky about her reading material, so though this whimsical choice surprised me, I trusted her judgment.

We were sitting in the reading nook of my shop, *Penny Pincher Used Books*. Please don't assume I'd actually named the store after myself. My grandmother, the store's original owner, did me that dubious honor. So even though I cringed a little inside every time I heard the name, I couldn't bear to change it. I'm not clinging sadly to all my grandmother's old possessions, but I kept the shop name. Every time I heard it, I also thought of Gram.

I'd given Tripp, the object of my affection, the book information and he'd ordered himself a copy from

Amazon. It hadn't come in yet, but it didn't really matter; he had to be careful about what he read as well.

I stared at the book in her hands with trepidation. "The title's kind of corny, isn't it?"

"It's fairly genre standard. You can't take paranormal romance too seriously, after all." Bobbie jutted her chin out a little defensively.

"No, no. That's fine. I trust your judgment."

Bobbie pursed her lips.

"All right! Let's do this thing!" Peter, Bobbie's boyfriend said with surprising enthusiasm.

"Hold up a minute; let me go over it one more time. I know I'm the novice vampire hunter, and Tripp's the vampire. Who will everyone else be?" I asked. Tripp was actually super-excited about his role. He looked forward to having super strength and speed—the fangs, not so much. We weren't yet sure if any of the supernatural stuff would actually work, so I hoped Tripp wouldn't be too disappointed if he was just a regular human-strength vampire.

"Other than the main characters, sometimes it's hard to know, so all I can do is guess. Peter will either be the werewolf in wolf form for the first chapter, or Thorne, the other vampire hunter. I'm not sure if I'll not show up or be cast in a male role. Normally, I'd be the wolf handler, but she's not in this scene. This will be an interesting experiment," Bobbie enthused.

Rolling my eyes, I took the book from her and turned it over. The cover was matte black and a blurb on the back told about the story. I was careful not to read any of it, lest we be pulled into the plot before we were ready. There was still much about the legacy magic we didn't understand, most of which we were learning the hard way. Every. Time.

The front listed the title and author's name, Hillary Shannon, along with the moon in the background, taking up most of the cover. On the bottom left portion of the cover a wolf silhouette howled at the moon opposite the silhouettes of two people running. I couldn't really judge the book by its cover, I didn't have anything to compare it with. I assumed it was pretty standard for this type of genre.

I did look up Hillary Shannon, but she hadn't published anything else and didn't even have an author web page. Maybe she was some kind of dark horse like the sparkly vampire author, and *Chase the Night* would end up being some kind of phenomenon. After this, I think I'd be pretty qualified to give her a review.

"Are we ready, then?" Bobbie asked.

"As I'll ever be. Here goes." I cracked the spine and turned to page one.

Chase the Night
Stacia closely followed Thorne into the cave. The wolf leading them stayed several yards ahead. The waves crashing behind them faded as they rounded corner after corner until only the sound of their footsteps and soft breaths remained.

The wolf slowed and Thorne did as well, raising his hand to keep Stacia behind him. He pulled his dagger from its sheath. This wasn't just any dagger. The Hunter's dagger, passed to Thorne from his father, and his father before him. Carved from a solid piece of hornbeam, the wood had been honed as sharp as any metal blade. It was oiled and cared for like a steel blade

168

as well, and it never failed. The patina gleamed, picking up and reflecting the faint light from Stacia's flashlight. Had it been daylight, you could have seen the stain of ancient blood on the blade.

"You must be far enough away that your prey cannot sense you, yet close enough to move in before the *were* loses control and tears the parasite to bits. 'Tis its nature. If the werewolf draws blood, even we won't be able to stop it." Thorne softly instructed Stacia.

"I may be a novice, but I'm not an imbecile," she retorted in a whisper. "I know the shifter's nature from my first year of training." The species that could change from human to animal form preferred to be called *shifters*, but old-school Thorne continued to call them werewolves, or simply *weres*. He was too arrogant to care about being politically correct, despite the invaluable assistance they provided Hunters.

Thorne glared at her in the weak light. He relished his role as instructor, the responsibility of imparting his vast wealth of knowledge to new Hunters. Had he married, he would be training his own son or daughter by now. Their demand so high, fewer Hunters were taking the time to start families of their own. With fewer Hunters by bloodline available, it was important that the knowledge and skills be passed to recruits thoroughly and precisely.

Ignoring her comment, Thorne focused his attention back to the wolf, who stopped, but stood on alert. Its stance indicated that it was safe to approach, for now. Stacia turned on her watch; in fifteen minutes the sun would set. They were safe for the time being but would have to hurry. This vampire was old, and wily. It was very possible that the darkness of the caves allowed it to waken earlier than younger demons.

"Xavier, we must take him alive. We must discover how far his network extends, and we can't do that if he's dead," Thorne spoke to the wolf, who responded with a low, irritated growl.

Stacia wanted to reach out and stroke the beast's fluffy neck but knew it would be unprofessional and unappreciated; he wasn't a dog, after all, or even a wolf most of the time.

"Come," Thorne said softly. Stacia tightened her grip on the kit bag and followed. This was the most dangerous thing a Hunter could do, surprise a vampire in its lair. A vampire was most vulnerable during the day when it slept. The Hunters planned to get in and incapacitate it before it woke. Usually, a lair would be protected by traps or the vampire's drudge, but this vamp was known to be a loner. It protected itself by constantly moving. Thorne had been tracking it for years.

Stacia felt vulnerable with her hands occupied by the flashlight and kit. She trusted Thorne and his experience to keep her safe. Thorne moved forward; the wolf stayed at her side. He was here for protection as well as tracking. Stacia shone her light ahead so Thorne could see and carefully followed.

After several more turns, the passage opened into a giant cavern, originally carved out by the ocean. The waves hadn't reached this far back in centuries, and the rocks that littered the floor were remarkably dry. Perfect for a vampire nap.

Thorne reached back and took the flashlight from Stacia's hand. He swept it slowly around the cavern, starting low and working his way up. The space looked to be one hundred feet wide and perhaps forty in depth. Falling rocks reshaped the perimeter, which had probably not been smooth to begin with.

The shadows hung deep beyond Thorne's moving light. There were too many places a vampire could tuck itself away. While the Hunter searched with his eyes, Xavier tested the air. He padded next to Thorne and nudged him to the left. Thorne concentrated in that direction, taking cautious steps forward, following the wolf. Stacia hung back. She silently unzipped the kit and pulled out the banded steel restraints, taking care they didn't clank. Thorne and the wolf rounded a stone formation the size of a truck and disappeared from view. Suddenly the silent cavern echoed with sounds of scuffling, hissing, and growls.

"Stacia, to me!" Thorne shouted. Penny grabbed the kit and hurried to her mentor. Without killing it, they wouldn't be able to hold the vamp for long. She rounded the rocks and found the vamp on his knees. Thorne stood behind him with blade poised at his quarry's pale neck. His face was flushed from exertion and a lock of graying hair now brushed the cheekbone below one penetrating blue eye. His biceps bulged, straining to hold his quarry. The wolf stood, teeth bared, with his claws digging into the vampire's impressive chest.

The vampire, rather than looking angry, had a bemused expression on its face. Tripp tensed when his prisoner reached into its own mouth and prodded at the elongated canines protruding from its gums.

"Duuuude, fangs!"

"Peter?!" I asked. *What the heck happened?*

****

"Penny?" Tripp removed the knife from Peter's neck and shook his hair out of his face.

"I thought you were supposed to be the vampire." I looked from Tripp to the wolf. "Bobbie?" The wolf just continued to growl at Peter.

"Hey, Fido, chill with the claws, would ya?" Peter attempted to remove the giant paws pressing into his chest.

"I take it this isn't going quite as planned," Tripp said. He sheathed his blade and bent to help Peter with his wolf problem. The wolf allowed it this time, then sat down with its tongue lolling out of its mouth.

"Bobbie!" I called, because the Bobbie I knew would never let her tongue hang like that.

"Penny!"

I looked around. Tripp peered at the ceiling, trying to locate Bobbie. Peter was trying out his new vampire-fast ninja moves. I ignored his nonchalance regarding his missing girlfriend.

"Where are you?" I called, my voice echoing through the cavern.

"I...I don't know. I don't think I'm anywhere, but I can see you and I can see the words on the pages of the book...oh, no," Bobbie's voice groaned. "I'm the narrator!"

"Say what?"

"I'm the narrator; I read everything that isn't dialogue, like an audio book, but with the characters having their own speaking parts."

"That's never happened before," Tripp and I said at the same time. We were both peering up, as if that's where Bobbie's disembodied voice came from. Peter stopped his ninja imitation and went back to poking at his fangs.

"How?" Tripp asked.

"I'm not sure...," Bobbie answered hesitantly. I sensed evasion.

"And I thought you said Tripp would be the vampire, the main character and love interest. How's that supposed to work now? I'll have scenes with Peter instead. No offense, but eww."

"None taken, Penn. You're like my sister or something," Peter added, though clearly not as disturbed by the series of events as Tripp and me.

"So if I'm this Thorne guy, what's my role?" Tripp asked, moving closer to me, but keeping an eye on the wolf, who sat scratching its unmentionables.

"Let me think for a minute," Bobbie pleaded.

"Babe," Peter called to the ceiling. "You just need to come clean; no one will be mad. They'll be proud of you, like I am." He gave us a hard look that dared us to do otherwise.

"Argh! Peter! Fine." I'd never heard Bobbie so rattled. "Penny, I'm so sorry, I should have told you, but I'm Hillary Shannon."

Tripp sent me a questioning look.

"The author?" I asked, trying to wrap my brain around what she was saying.

"Yes, I'm the author. I had no idea any of this would happen. I think because I wrote the story, the magic cast me as the narrator. And I guess since I created the main character with my own personal love interest in mind, Peter got cast as the vampire."

Tripp held up his hands. "Whoa, whoa, hold up. How did you write and get this published so fast? We've only been doing this a few months."

"Bobbie's been writing for a long time. Last year I finally talked her into publishing some of it." Peter's chest puffed with pride.

"How come you never told me? This is kind of a big deal." I couldn't believe she hadn't shared this with me. She was my best friend—she knew all about my family curse and everything. It hurt.

"I'm sorry, Penny; so, so sorry. I didn't mean to keep it from you, but my writing is fluff. I'm having trouble being proud of the accomplishment while being embarrassed by the content. It's not even the kind of thing I enjoy reading. I tried reading a couple different light fiction genres to help me relax, but some of the plots were so ridiculous, I couldn't focus. I started writing because I felt like it wouldn't be hard to do a better job. Eventually, instead of reading, I found myself writing romantic fiction to relax."

"So the whole bit about you reading this book and loving it was all a lie?"

I could sense her cringing even if I couldn't see her. "It's the one I thought was good enough to publish."

"How much of that decision has to do with my situation?" I asked. Tripp was right; we hadn't been dealing with the legacy long enough for Bobbie to have created a whole story for me.

"I've had this one written for a little over a year now. Once we figured out what you were dealing with, I started the publishing process. I'd honestly hoped it would provide us with more control."

Tripp snorted.

"I am proud of you. It's very cool that you've published a book. I'm just shocked." I gave Tripp a reproachful look.

"So, madam narrator, what do we need to do to finish out this scene?" Tripp asked, trying, almost successfully, to mask the annoyance in his voice. His irritated expression gave him away, though.

"Um, the vampire, Lucien, and Stacia lock eyes and make a connection. You, Thorne, restrain him and escort him to the Hunters' containment headquarters."

I glanced at Peter, currently trying to crush a rock in the palm of his hand. "Gotcha," I said. "But that first part isn't going to happen."

"All right, let's go." Tripp shined the light in the direction we'd come from and stalked off. The rest of us could follow or stand around in the dark. The wolf trailed behind, occasionally nipping at Peter's heels.

I caught up to Tripp and snagged his empty hand in mine. "I'll call you tonight, okay?"

"Sure," he said shortly, but let go of my hand to wrap his arm around my shoulders. He squeezed me and kissed the top of my head. This was an unusual turn of events, in already beyond unusual circumstances. All we could do was roll with it.

A word about the author...

Shelley is a twenty-five-year resident of Oklahoma with roots in Maine. She and her husband have four awesome kids but are thrilled three have successfully reached adulthood and moved out. She spends her time working with students, writing, reading, baking, sewing, and exercising just enough to counteract her other activities.

Always willing to escape into the plot of a good book, she hopes her Penny series offers a similar escape to her readers.

www.shelleywhitewrites.com
https://www.facebook.com/shelleywhiteauthor/
https://www.goodreads.com/author/show/21635067.Shelley_White
https://www.bookbub.com/authors/shelley-white